Venom

Nikki Tate

orca sports

ORCA BOOK PUBLISHERS

Library and Archives Canada Cataloguing in Publication

Tate, Nikki, 1962-
Venom / written by Nikki Tate.

(Orca sports)
ISBN 978-1-55469-071-8

I. Title. II. Series.
PS8589.A8735V45 2009   jC813'.54   C2008-907420-3

Summary: Spencer is sure someone is doping the racehorses
at the stable where he works, but no one will listen to him
until he gets some proof.

First published in the United States, 2009
Library of Congress Control Number: 2008941143

Orca Book Publishers gratefully acknowledges the support for its publishing
programs provided by the following agencies: the Government of Canada
through the Book Publishing Industry Development Program and the
Canada Council for the Arts, and the Province of British Columbia through
the BC Arts Council and the Book Publishing Tax Credit.

Cover design by Teresa Bubela
Cover photography by Getty Images
Author photo by E. Colin Williams

Orca Book Publishers   Orca Book Publishers
PO Box 5626, Stn. B   PO Box 468
Victoria, BC Canada   Custer, WA USA
V8R 6S4   98240-0468

www.orcabook.com
Printed and bound in Canada.
Printed on 100% PCW.

12 11 10 09 • 4 3 2 1

For Cyd, muck bucket queen

chapter one

"You're fired!"

I step back and kick over a feed bucket. The horses answer with a chorus of whinnies. They're expecting breakfast.

"After you clean up that mess!" Scampy spins away from me and stalks off.

"You can't—" I yell at the trainer's back.

Scampy wheels around. His face is purple and the veins in his temples look like they might pop.

"I can do what I want. This barn"—he waves his arm at the horses on both sides of the wide aisle—"this barn has room for one trainer. And that trainer would be me!" Scampy jabs his thumb into his chest and bugs out his eyes. Then his jaw starts working. *Chomp. Chomp.* He mashes his fat wad of gum like he wants to destroy it.

"Understand?"

There's no chance to answer. Scampy is gone. The sound of his cowboy boots clicking on the concrete fades as he stomps off down the barn aisle and around the corner.

"What was that all about?" Em steps out of the tack room behind me. It's chilly this time of the morning. She's wearing one of those wool caps with earflaps and a pom-pom.

"Your uncle just fired me." I'm impressed by how calm I sound. I've never been fired before.

"What did you do?"

"Nothing. Why do you always have to take his side?" I've worked for Jacob "Scampy"

Scallopini's Racing Stable for a little more than a year. Em's been here forever. Her parents own a couple of horses, but it's her Uncle Scampy who is always at the barn.

Em tips her head to the side, making her pom-pom swing.

"Scampy wouldn't fire you for nothing."

My gaze slides over to the big bay gelding whose head pokes out of his stall. Lord of the Fires watches us intently, waiting for someone to start feeding him.

"Spencer, you are an idiot," Em says. "There is nothing wrong with Lordy."

My jaw clamps shut. There *is* something wrong with Lord of the Fires. I'm his main exercise rider, and I know. The horse hasn't felt right for weeks.

"How did he do on Saturday?" Em asks, her fists jammed against her hips. "Hmmm?"

She doesn't really expect an answer. I don't give her one. We both know that Lordy ran well. He came in second, just behind the favorite.

"What did you say to Scampy?"

The scene replays in my head. I had arrived at 4:30 AM to start work. The lights were on and Scampy was already here. He came out of Lordy's stall and slipped something—a syringe, maybe—into his pocket. All I did was ask what he'd given the horse. I didn't say the words *illegal doping*. I didn't say anything about cheating. I asked a simple question. *What did you just give the horse?*

That's when Scampy lost it. That's how I got fired.

"Well?" Em demands.

"Nothing. I didn't say a thing."

Em sniffs and tosses her head. "Fine. Be like that. Scampy will tell me."

She marches off, leaving me to sweep up the mess of spilled grain.

How can it be that my day is already going so badly? It isn't even 5:00 AM!

I fetch a broom and start sweeping. The short conversation with Scampy and the longer one with Em repeat in my head.

"So the old man gave you the boot?" Tony Harper, Scampy's other groom, shows up as I sweep up the last of the grain.

4

"Word travels fast," I say.

Tony folds his beefy arms across his chest. "I heard Scampy talking to Em outside the barn. Want some advice?"

I don't. Tony gives me some anyway. "You're a good rider, Spencer. And people know you're a good worker; they like it when you help out."

I sense there's a *but* coming.

"But you have to learn when to keep your mouth shut and your nose out of other people's business."

Tony reaches out to give my shoulder a squeeze. His hand rests there a little longer than it needs to. When he squeezes, it hurts. I'm careful not to let anything show in my face. Tony doesn't need to know that he creeps me out. He doesn't need to know how ticked off I am. Or how worried.

Word does travel fast here in the barns at Hilltop Racetrack. Most people never see the backside of the track. It's like a world of its own. The last thing I need is to get a reputation as a troublemaker in this tight community.

I force myself to smile. "Thanks, Tony. I'll keep that in mind."

"You do that," he says as he releases his grip on my shoulder. It feels more like he just gave me a warning than a friendly piece of advice.

After I finish cleaning up the grain spill, I figure it's best if I leave. I hop on my bike and start for home. The ride only takes six and a half minutes, but I'm not even halfway there when my cell phone rings.

"Get your ass back here."

"Scampy?"

"Who else would it be? You're late for work."

"Does this mean I'm un-fired?"

"You're on probation."

That's all he says. No apology. No explanation. Then the line goes dead.

Getting un-fired makes me almost as mad as getting fired. Who does he think he is? I nearly keep on pedaling.

What makes me turn the bike around is the horses. The riding. The races. And, if I'm really honest, Em.

I might love the track, but I make a promise to myself as I pedal up to Scampy's shedrow. If he is doing something illegal with Lord of the Fires, I'm going to find out what it is. Then he'll be sorry for firing me—and even sorrier he hired me back.

chapter two

I hiss at Chiquita Manana and crouch low over her neck. The three-year-old filly kicks into another gear. All the tension I felt back at the barn evaporates as we speed up. We hug the rail and shoot past the crowd of trainers watching their horses run in the soft misty glow of the early morning workout. The filly's breath comes in short punches, timed exactly with the *thud-thud-thud* of each big stride.

The beat of the Thoroughbred's hooves drives my heart rate through the roof. There's nothing quite like the lift and thrust of a thousand pounds of muscle pulsing beneath me.

Chiquita doesn't need much encouragement. My hands move back and forth on either side of her neck. I'm in perfect rhythm with the galloping horse. We move easily around the final turn, and I let her go.

We flash past Scampy's red and black jacket. I can't see the stopwatch in his hand, but I know it's there. I gasp for breath as if I've just finished a fast workout myself. Easing back a touch, I let the big chestnut filly know it's time to slow down.

The horse's neck is slick and dark with sweat. She pulls against me. She wants to keep running. I guide her away from the rail, still moving at a healthy clip. She tosses her head, fussing, when I suggest she slows.

We communicate through muscle and tendon and bone. From hand to leather reins to bit to mouth and back again. Human to horse, horse to human. Our conversation lasts halfway around the track. Finally I insist it's time to steady and slow. Chiquita insists she'd rather keep playing than head back to the barn.

I know what she means. It's 7:30 AM, and despite all that's happened this morning, I'm not looking forward to the end of my shift. Leaving the track means I have to start my day all over again with morning classes at Reston High.

"Not bad, not bad," Scampy says, meeting us at the gate. As usual, one cheek bulges with grape bubblegum. "Damn, she's a nice-moving filly. How'd she feel?"

Scampy has been like this ever since I got back to the barn. It's like nothing happened. Would it have killed him to apologize? Or does he think being nice will convince me he didn't do anything wrong?

Chiquita dances lightly beneath me, her neck arched, feet barely touching the ground. She's still excited, breathing hard.

Well, two can play at being nice.

"She felt good," I say. "Fast. Strong. She's a good filly."

Scampy has a chew on his wad of gum and then shifts the bulge to his other cheek.

"Em's waiting inside with Caravaggio. Nice and slow for him. He's racing two weeks from Sunday—and he's been going good. Then I'll get you to do Big Bad Billy. Same as yesterday. Then you're good to go. You don't want to be late for school, do you?"

He slaps Chiquita's backside a bit harder than he needs to. She squirts forward into a jog.

Back in the barn, I slide off Chiquita and hand her off to Em. Tony gives me a leg up on Caravaggio. I avoid Tony's eyes and resist the urge to wipe my knee where he touched me. Caravaggio is already moving off along the shedrow while I find my stirrups, organize my reins and get settled for another gallop, my seventh this morning.

I reach forward and run my knuckles along Caravaggio's neck. My back and shoulders ache, and there's a spot on the inside of my left knee that's rubbed raw. I've been fired and un-fired and almost had a fight with Em. Yeah, it's tough some days at the track, but there's no place I'd rather be.

chapter three

On Saturday, Grandma nearly scares the crap out of me when she pops her head into my room before I'm even awake and asks, "Who do you like better in the third? Cinnamon Puff, Whoyourdaddy or Spideylegs?"

"What time is it?"

"Just after four. I didn't hear any noise in here. I thought you might have overslept."

"Thanks. I was just waking up."

I roll over and stretch. "I like Cinnamon Puff. She blew past me a couple of weeks ago."

"Thank you, love."

The door closes softly behind her. I pull the covers back over my head for another few minutes. It's still dark. Normal teen-agers are barely getting into bed after a Friday night of hard partying. And me? It's four in the morning and I'm giving my grandmother hot tips for today's races!

When I drag myself down into the kitchen, Grandma's got a pot of coffee on and the race program printed out from the computer. It's already marked up with her secret code. She highlights horses she likes in yellow, underlines jockeys who are winning with red and puts a big black X beside a horse or rider she really doesn't like.

There's at least one race each day she leaves up to Lady Luck. That one she marks in green and always bets on the number seven, no matter who's riding what horse. She's been playing her system for a thousand years.

"What do you think of Majestic Ensign?"

I pull a face, and Grandma puts a black X beside Majestic Ensign's name.

I pour a little coffee into my thermos, slap PB&J on some bread and shrug into my jacket. "Good luck at the races!" I yell over my shoulder as I jog out the door.

The bike ride to the track takes just enough time to get me warmed up and fully awake. I wonder sometimes how things would have been different if Grandma's house had been on the other side of town, away from the track. As it is, my earliest memories are of my mom dropping me off at Grandma's for weekend visits.

Grandma and I used to head straight for the track to watch the races. It was especially exciting on days when my dad had horses running. Even before the accident, Mom rarely came with us. After the accident, nobody could even say the word *track* without Mom losing it.

In the past few years, Mom and Grandma have had some unbelievable fights about the place that cannot be named. They almost always ended with my mom screaming, "How can you do this to me? Don't put me through that again!"

I know my mom has good reasons to hate the track. At some point, though, she needs to realize I am not my dad. What happened to him won't happen to me.

I can't think about the accident, even though it happened six years ago. If I do, it makes me want to puke. That's not how I like to remember my dad. It's bad enough that the accident haunts my nightmares. I don't need it to ruin the daytime too. That's what happens when you dwell on the past. Too bad Mom doesn't see things that way.

Things got really bad the summer I turned twelve, two years after the accident. I was staying at Grandma's one weekend, and she made some comment about how wrong it was for Mom to let her boyfriend sleep over. It sort of slipped out just as we were finishing ice-cream cones at the park. That part wasn't so strange, I guess. Grandma has always worried about Mom.

My reaction, though, was definitely off the wall.

I started bawling. Blubbering like a baby. When Grandma asked what was wrong, the words gushed out. I couldn't stop them. I told her how miserable Mom was, how many days she stayed in her bedroom with the door locked. I told Grandma how I found empty liquor bottles under the couch and hidden under the newspapers in the recycling bin, and how Mom made me call her work to say she was too sick to come in.

I even showed her the bruises on my arm where Mom had grabbed me.

Through it all, Grandma just listened. When I was done, she said, "I think you need a place of your own to go."

"Like a tree house?"

"A tree house? You're a bit old for that, aren't you?"

Grandma had something quite different planned. "You need somewhere you can go and hang out and make yourself useful. Somewhere away from your mother.

Somewhere away from me. Somewhere to be yourself." The next thing I knew, we were at the security gate leading to the backside of the track, where all the barns are. Grandma asked for Little Joe.

Little Joe (no relation to Big Joe, who's just a big jerk) is the trainer who gave me my first job as a hot walker. Grandma fudged my age a little. And she agreed that we didn't need to tell Mom right away, at least not while she was going through such a rough patch.

The new job worked out well for a while. I earned a little pocket money on weekends when I stayed with Grandma. Lots of the people I met had known my dad, and somehow that made him seem closer. Grandma was happy. She had someone on the backside to give her tips about which horses were sore, which horses were training well, what the trainers were saying in the barn aisles. It was a great setup.

Until Mom found out. She screamed and swore and slammed me against the kitchen doorframe.

"How could you do this to me?" she yelled, throwing me sideways. "You don't care what I think! You ungrateful–" Mom grabbed the coffeepot off the counter and flung it at me. The glass pot hit the floor and shattered. Hot coffee spattered every-where, stinging my skin where it splashed on my arms. Gary, the guy she was dating at the time, stepped in. He wrapped his arms around her from behind, but could barely hold her back.

"Get out!" he said to me, jabbing his chin in the direction of the door. "Go!"

I headed for Grandma's. Where else was I going to go?

That was three years ago, two weeks after my thirteenth birthday. I haven't lived with my mom since.

When I first moved in, Grandma thought maybe we'd made a mistake getting me a job at the track. But I'd say it was the best idea Grandma has ever had. I did need a place of my own to go, somewhere away from Mom and her booze and her boyfriends. The only time I see Mom is when she has a parenting moment and shows up at Grandma's. Christmas, my birthday and Thanksgiving usually mean a visit. So does a phone call from my school. That's why I actually show up there on most days. I sure don't go because I like the place.

Living with Grandma is a good arrangement. As long as I more or less keep out of trouble and keep feeding her tips, we get along great. So far, we've never had an awkward hole in a conversation. As long as the Thoroughbreds are running at Hilltop Racetrack, I don't suppose we ever will.

chapter four

"Hey, Em," I say. "Where's Scampy?"

Ever since the firing incident, I like to keep track of Scampy. I try to get an idea of how his day is going before I talk to him. We have a truce. I don't say anything he could take the wrong way. He doesn't pick on me any more than he picks on anyone else. I know something is going on with Lordy. I keep my eyes open and my thoughts to myself.

"Scampy left about ten minutes ago. He's picking up that horse from Johnson's farm. Check the board."

The whiteboard in Scampy's tack room is the master plan. All the horses he's training are listed down the left. Beside each one he's written instructions for the day. *Walk only. Walk jog. Slow gallop. Turnout 60 mins.* There's a spot for feed, a place to write supplements, and notes about everything from bandaging to equipment changes to medication doses.

I don't need to worry about anything except what's in the exercise-ride column. He's assigned numbers to the horses that need to be worked this morning, and I know he likes them to go in the right order.

Tony and Em get here even earlier than I do. They've been busy this morning. The fourteen horses Scampy trains have all been fed and watered.

Lordy is the first horse on the ride list. I wonder if it's a test. Maybe Scampy has left instructions with Em to keep an eye on me. She'll probably report everything I say.

Lord of the Fires has already been groomed. Tony comes out of a stall just as I come out of the tack room.

"Lordy looks good," I say, careful to sound casual.

"He's a good horse," Tony says, giving Lordy a pat on the neck.

Em nods and checks the girth.

I fasten my helmet buckle with a snap.

"Take it easy," Tony says to me. It's an innocent enough thing to say, but something about the way Tony smirks makes me wonder what he means. Is everyone spying and ready to report back to Scampy?

Em laces her fingers together and I bend my left leg. She cups my knee in her hands and we count—*one*, *two*, *three*. Em might not be big, but she's strong. With my jump and her push, I'm in the saddle as if I weighed nothing.

Lord of the Fires doesn't wait. He's an old pro and all business as he strides off. Horses pop their heads over their stall doors and watch us go by. At the end of our row I look left, wait for a gap in the horse traffic and call out, "Horse moving in!" We slip into the procession heading for the track.

Post time for the first race is 2:00 PM. The horses that aren't racing still need their workouts. It's like a carnival every morning, with horses coming and going. Golf carts and bicycles zip around the maze of barns. Grooms and stable hands scurry this way and that, pushing wheelbarrows piled high with manure or bales of hay. Trainers yell instructions and rude jokes in about equal doses. A few jockeys and their agents hang around, meeting with trainers and checking out horses the jockeys will ride later in the day.

"Hey, Spencer, you gonna stop growing any time soon?" Fletcher, an older guy who does more work these days as a gallop boy than he does as a jockey, is always giving me a hard time about my height. He's riding one of Chester MacGuire's horses, a big black colt with a brilliant white blaze and four evenly matched white socks. Fletcher pulls up beside me. He continues his ribbing as we make our way to the gate at the back of the track.

For a while last summer, I prayed that maybe I'd get lucky and never grow. Jockeys are about the only people who think that way. Right around Christmas, Grandma and I were horrified to discover all my jeans were too short.

I'm as skinny as ever, but already too tall to hope to be a jockey. But I can still work the horses, keeping them in shape and getting them ready to race. That's almost as good.

Fletcher and I ride through the gate together, and then he takes off at a fast canter, his horse glossy and well-muscled. Lord of the Fires waits until I ask, and then lifts into a long, reaching trot. No sign of soreness. He's moving easily and seems relaxed. We keep to the outside, giving up the inside to the horses having fast workouts. I cluck to Lordy and he picks up to a canter. We gather speed as we move around the track.

Every fiber of my body is tuned to the horse. Have I imagined he hasn't been himself?

I don't want him to be lame, but I don't want to be wrong either. I've felt him hesitate when I've pushed him hard and when we've worked fast through the turns. Right now, though, he feels okay.

I'm not even aware of when it happens, when I slip into my riding bubble and the rest of the world disappears. Today the bubble pops practically before it forms when the alarm buzzer sounds. A voice over the loudspeaker warns, "Loose horse! Heads up! Loose horse!"

chapter five

"Whoa...easy..."

I concentrate all my attention on Lord of the Fires. *Stay calm.* When the riderless gray horse tears past us, head up and eyes wild, a ripple of crazy energy radiates from Lordy. I grab hold of his mane. He gives a hearty buck and bolts off after the loose horse. Somehow, I manage to stay on.

I'm vaguely aware of riders trying to keep their horses under control and out of the way. Ahead, one of the track outriders heads off the gray. The horse wheels around and gallops straight toward us.

I haul on Lordy, trying to pull his head around. He clamps down on the bit and ignores me. The loose horse charges past us. Lordy hits the brakes, and I fly up onto his neck. It's all I can do to hang on. Lordy spins so we are facing the other direction. I *thunk* back into the saddle. I've lost both my stirrups. Lordy races off after the gray. Someone shouts as we whip past.

Ahead, several people on foot have formed a line across the track. They wave their arms in the air. At first I think the gray is going to plow right into them. At the last second the horse turns back toward the outrider, who passes me, yelling, "Pull up! Pull up!"

I haul on Lordy's left rein and drive my bootheel into his left side. My arm muscles feel like they're going to rip. Finally I pull Lordy into a small circle.

A man runs over and catches hold of Lordy's bridle. The horse flings his head up, half rearing.

"You okay?" the guy who has hold of Lordy's bridle asks.

Lordy snorts. He skitters sideways as we try to get him under control. He isn't paying much attention to either of us. Lordy's head jerks up and his ears prick forward, intent on the gray, who has been caught by the outrider. The outrider's dun-colored Quarter Horse is completely calm despite the stupid behavior of the young Thoroughbred.

"Easy, nutbar," the guy on the ground says to Lordy.

I nudge my toes back into the stirrups and get a better grip on the reins with my left hand. The fingers of my right hand are still twisted through Lordy's wild mane. Lord of the Fires feels like he could explode at any moment. Stripes of white lather mark sweaty lines where the reins run alongside his neck.

"Settle down, settle down," the guy on the ground murmurs through clenched teeth.

"Let him go," I say. The gray has been led away. I'm pretty sure that if I can let Lordy move again, he'll feel happier. For all Lordy knows, the gray was escaping from a saber-toothed tiger, and the only sensible thing to do was run away. We humans like to think we are in charge, but horses are big strong prey animals. Their best defense is to run faster than whatever is chasing them. God help the rider who thinks it's actually possible to reason with a horse in flight mode.

"Let go!" I say again.

"You sure?"

"I'm fine." My heart hammers in my chest. "I'm fine," I repeat a little louder. Some of the other riders have started moving again, even though the all-clear buzzer hasn't sounded. I'm not the only one having trouble controlling my horse.

Over on the outside rail, Angie and Taylor, two riders from Doc Masters' barn, are walking their mounts in small circles. Just being close to the other horses seems to calm Lord of the Fires. He lets out a loud whinny that nearly shakes me out of the saddle. Angie and Taylor see my death grip on the mane and laugh. It's not a mean laugh, more like the kind of laugh that happens after you nearly die, but don't.

"Crazy mare, that gray," Angie says.

"Don't know why Geoff bothers to keep her in training," Taylor adds. "She's got a brain the size of a pea."

The all clear sounds, and the three of us turn our horses and pick up an easy canter on the outside rail. Inside, the faster horses are soon back in gear, manes and tails streaming behind them. We take it easy, Angie and Taylor chatting all the way around the track.

Lord of the Fires is eager enough to keep up, but the unevenness is back. I ask for a lead change so he's leading with his right leg instead of his left when he reaches forward in each stride. He gives me the change, but switches back on his own after just a few steps. After two laps, we pull up and I turn Lordy for the out gate. Now that we've slowed down, he feels okay again. What I know for certain is that I have not been imagining he's bordering on lame.

chapter six

There's quite a crowd at the gate. Trainers wait, asking if horse, then rider, is okay. Hands reach out to touch horses' sweaty necks and offer reassurance. Grooms stand ready to help take horses back to the barn. When the loose-horse alarm sounds, it's amazing how many people emerge from the barns—to see the damage, to pick up the pieces.

"You okay?"

Em is at Lordy's shoulder, her hand reaching up toward my knee.

My heart flutter kicks. Em looks genuinely worried. "How's Lordy? Did you see what happened?"

Maybe Em's just worried about the horse. "Don't know. It was that gray mare of Geoff O'Reilly's. Flipped out."

"Ryan Murray got carried off on a stretcher. He did something to his leg, I think. He couldn't stand on his own."

Legs heal, I think. It would have been worse if the rider had been unconscious. My stomach squeezes. White sheets. Bandages. The hiss of a machine squeezing air into someone's lungs.

"He'll be fine," I say quickly, pushing away the memories.

Lordy has decided it's time to head back to the barn. Em is keeping up beside us, half walking and half jogging.

"He might be a little off," I say. "After the gray bolted past us, we had some trouble. When we cantered, he seemed stiff or something."

Em scoots back a few steps and watches us. "Looks fine now. Are you sure?"

"I'm sure. I know what I felt."

"Because I can't save your sorry ass every time you have a bumpy ride."

Em hasn't missed too many chances to remind me that she's the one who convinced Scampy to hire me back. I don't push it. Em will do the right thing.

"I'll wrap Lordy after I cool him out," she says. "You're okay?"

"Yeah. Nothing like a jolt of adrenaline to wake a guy up."

Em laughs. "Coffee would work too. You want a cup? I don't want to put on another pot just for me."

"Sure. I'll grab a cup after I ride Chiquita."

It's a good thing Em sprints off between the barns. The minute the words are out of my mouth, heat rises in my cheeks. She doesn't need to know my thermos is still half-full. She certainly doesn't need to know that her offer of coffee makes me want to grin. I shut down the smile and turn my attention to getting Lordy back to the barn.

Whatever thought I might have had of a cozy cup of coffee in the tack room with Em quickly evaporates. Tony has his feet up on the truck bench in the tack room. The truck bench is one of several pieces of furniture that once had some other purpose. It's bolted to the floor beside a stack of milk crates. The top crate serves as an end table. The others are packed full of neatly rolled leg wraps, bottles of liniment and copies of *Thoroughbred Times* and *Blood Horse*.

Tony's eyes are closed, and he sounds like a sick diesel engine on a cold morning. The last thing I need to do is disturb his beauty rest.

The barns hum with activity. I rush to keep up with the horses that Em gets ready for me to ride. Scampy has also asked another exercise rider, Wee Jimmy Jump-up, to help. The spring meet is rolling along, and Scampy has increased the number of horses he wants worked each day. Tony reappears at some point, but he's in a sour mood. We all keep out of his way.

After I've ridden six horses, I'm ready for my lunch even though it isn't even nine. I'm munching my way through my sticky sandwich when I hear several loud bangs out in the aisle. Scampy yells, "Settle down in there!"

"Who's that?" I ask when a new dark bay horse with a narrow blaze sticks its head over the top of the stall door.

"Devil May Care. A Stunning Mate stud colt out of Pussy Winnow, a Black Kat mare from Johnson's farm."

Scampy speaks the language of bloodlines as easily as he breathes and chews gum. Stunning Mate is the name of a stallion in Ontario who sired a few decent horses before he had to be put down. He broke a back leg in a freak accident out in his paddock. I've never heard of the new horse's dam, Pussy Winnow. But I've certainly heard of Black Kat. He's one of a whole bunch of top-notch Thoroughbreds that can be traced back to a couple of Kentucky horses.

Both of those superstars have "Kat" in their names.

"Three-year-old," Scampy says before I have a chance to ask. "No experience. He had some damned infection last year, so he never raced. We'll get him going tomorrow."

Another boom sounds from the colt's stall as Devil May Care pounds the wall with a back hoof.

"Stop that!" Scampy scowls at the horse and picks up a broom. "I'll smack you a good one if you keep that up!"

The horse lets fly with another kick. Scampy whacks the outside of the stall door with the broom. The broom makes a loud noise, but doesn't hit the horse. Devil May Care pokes his head back over the half door and snorts.

"Don't think I like this horse," Scampy says as he puts the broom down. When he reaches over to touch Devil May Care's neck, the horse pulls his head back and retreats into his stall. "How were the rides today?"

I follow Scampy into the tack room and we go through the list, starting with Lord of the Fires. I hesitate and then say, "We had a little trouble. That gray mare of Geoff's bolted. Lordy sort of took off." I know there's no point in hiding what happened. Scampy's probably heard all the gory details seventeen times already.

"You shouldn't have let him get away from you like that," Scampy says.

"I know. But he—"

"Be ready next time. Em's got him wrapped?"

I nod.

"Anything else?"

For the first time, I don't tell Scampy everything. I don't mention Lordy was uneven. I want to keep my job.

"No—that's it."

Scampy narrows his eyes like he doesn't believe me. He doesn't push, though. "What about Chiquita?"

One by one I bring Scampy up to speed on what the rides were like. Chiquita was strong and relaxed. Twitter wanted to race

the big red four-year-old out of Doc Masters'
barn. Bing Bang Bong just wanted to nap.
"He's really lazy," I say. "It's like he has no
interest in what's going on."

"Dumb as a bag of hammers," Scampy
says. "I'll call Dr. Conrad and we'll see how
much longer she wants to keep him here."

Bing definitely lacks enthusiasm, but
I don't think the horse is dumb. He just
needs another job. I don't mind giving him
a bad report card, though. For one thing,
he hasn't placed in a race yet, so it's no
big secret he's a little short on talent. But I
also know that the owner, a lady vet from
Vernon, always takes her retired racehorses
to another trainer. The horses learn other
jobs that don't involve racing. I've heard
they usually wind up with pretty good
homes as show jumpers or eventers or pleasure horses. That's more than I can say for
some of the horses after their track careers
are done.

"Need a hand?" I ask Em, who is pushing
a wheelbarrow piled high with sacks of feed.

"I'd never say no to an offer like that," she says.

We unload and stack the feed. We fetch three more barrows loaded with heavy feed sacks from Scampy's truck before we take a break.

After that, I help Em fill the hay nets and top up the water buckets. Then I join Grandma in the stands to watch the races.

It's a fluky Saturday. Scampy doesn't have a horse running. It's great to be a spectator. Next weekend it will be all hands on deck. I won't have the luxury of sitting down for a whole afternoon.

chapter seven

A couple of weeks later, Grandma and I are at the kitchen table.

"Spencer—where's your head?" Grandma glares at me. "I asked if you wanted another spud."

"Sorry. Yeah."

"Yeah?"

"Yes, please."

Grandma drops the baked potato onto my plate. "What's on your mind?"

Em. Em. Em. I'm not about to tell my grandmother that I can't get a girl out of my mind. Ever since the day when Geoff O'Reilly's gray mare messed up my morning, I've looked at Em differently. Which is dumb, because she's still her old, slightly snotty self. But she had reached up to touch my knee. That moment was the highlight of my month.

"Girl trouble?" Grandma winks and pushes the gravy jug across the table.

"No." Fortunately, the Lordy problem is getting more complicated so my quick response isn't exactly a lie. "Are you ready for tomorrow?" I ask, changing the subject.

"Working on it as we speak." Grandma fishes several sheets of paper out of a stack she's pushed aside to make room for the dinner dishes. She slides the list of tomorrow's race entries across the table toward me. She has also printed out Billy Bob's Picks. Billy Bob is one of several race handicappers who offer advice to people like

Grandma. Grandma figures he's the best in the business.

I point at the fifth race. "Lordy's running."

"Lord of the Fires?" She puts on her reading glasses and studies the race information. "Six furlongs. Nick Espinoza is riding. He's been doing okay recently. Claiming race: $25,000. What do you think?"

"He shouldn't be racing."

Grandma peers over her reading glasses and raises her eyebrows. "Espinoza or the horse?"

"The horse. He's still not right. He was the one I was riding the day that gray mare got loose. He felt awful." Awful is a bit strong, but I don't want Grandma to lose her money betting on a horse I know won't be near the winners.

"I'm sure Scampy knows what he's doing."

I pour a healthy dose of thick gravy over my baked potato. "They've been looking after him okay, I guess. Em's been icing and wrapping his legs. But I rode him a week ago and he's still not himself. When I asked him for speed, it was like he just wasn't that interested. He was sort of uneven in the turns—not strong and smooth like he used to be."

Grandma mashes some peas into her potato and loads up a forkful.

"It's not like he's seriously lame or anything. I rode him twice last week and again on Monday. But he's not right. I can feel it."

"Horses aren't machines. They have good days; they get sour."

"I know that. But he was pretty consistent last season. This summer it's like he's always being careful, not going all out."

"What does Scampy say?"

How do I answer *that*? Grandma doesn't need to know Scampy fired me for questioning how he was treating the horse. "Scampy has his own way of doing things."

Grandma slides her reading glasses down her nose and gives me a hard look.

"Yesterday Wee Jimmy Jump-up rode Lordy," I say.

"And? What did Jimmy say?"

"He'd never say anything against Scampy. He actually said Lordy felt good! It doesn't make any sense." For a moment I consider telling Grandma about my suspicions that Scampy is doping the horse. She wouldn't appreciate it. Scampy and Grandma go way back. Back to the Dad days.

Grandma puts the tip of her pen beside Lord of the Fires' name. "So—what do you think?"

"He shouldn't be running. If Scampy doesn't scratch him, I'd say you'd be wasting your money to bet on him."

Grandma puts a big black X beside Lordy's name. "Who do you like in the seventh?" she asks. We spend the rest of the meal trying to predict the unpredictable.

On Saturday Em and I stand elbow to elbow at the rail, squinting into the sun as the horses barrel around the final turn and charge down the backstretch. Two horses are neck and neck, running stride for stride toward the finish line. A big bay is closing the gap, but looks to be too far back to catch the leaders. The rest of the field straggles behind the others. Not that we care about the stragglers. Lord of the Fires is one of the two leaders!

"Go, Lordy!" Em yells, as if the horse might hear her over the roar of the crowd. "Go! Go! Go!" She pumps the air with her fist. When the other horse gives a huge final effort in the last three strides and pulls just ahead of Lordy, she slumps forward. "Ohhh. So close!"

The announcer calls out the names and numbers of the top three horses, and the payout amounts flash up onto the odds board. Lordy ran at 12:1 odds. If someone bet two bucks on him to win and he had won, they'd get twenty-four bucks back. Even though he came second, it still wasn't a bad payout. I feel a twinge of guilt when I think of my bad advice to Grandma. Apparently, Scampy knows his horse better than I do.

Em punches me in the shoulder.

"Ow!" I rub my arm. "What was that for?"

"I knew he'd run a good race," Em says. "Sorry. Didn't mean to hit you so hard."

"We'd better hustle," I say, knowing Scampy will be expecting us. Tony is handling Lordy today. He's the one who will collect the horse in front of the grandstand. The horses are already making their way there. Jockeys hop off and have a quick consultation with trainers before they scoot off to get ready for another race.

"Don't be such a sore loser," Em says as we set off at a jog back toward the barn. The announcer indicates that Lord of the Fires has been randomly selected to go for drug testing. When Lordy gets back from the drug-testing barn, he'll need cooling out and a bath. This isn't officially part of my job, but I like hanging out with Em and giving her a hand.

"I'm not mad," I insist. And I'm not. But I am worried. I can't stop thinking about Scampy coming out of the stall with that syringe. I wonder if anything will show up in the drug tests.

"Race you to security," Em says. She takes off fast. Her feet pound down the gravel road leading to the security gate. I sprint to catch up and overtake her. My lungs burn. She's fast. I dig deep and run harder. I arrive at the security gate first and bend in half, resting my hands on my knees, puffing and blowing.

Em breezes past me, waves at Jo-Anne in the window and then slows to a walk. "You coming?" she calls over her shoulder. Even though I clearly won the race, the toss of her head and the way she strides off make me feel like I lost.

chapter eight

Ten days later, I'm back up on Lord of the Fires, crouched low over his neck. It's bucketing down rain, and I'm squinting so I can see where we're going. Mud flies up in my face. My goggles are soon smeared with muck.

One of the riders from Doc Masters' barn is on a pretty bay filly. They match us stride for stride as we move into the turn just past the grandstand. It's when we lean into the turn that I feel it again: hesitation when I ask the horse to maintain his speed. Coming out of the turn, he eases up just as I'm about to ask him to slow down. Did he sense I was going to ask? Or did he pull up because he's hurting again? Or is it the mucky footing? It's been a long time since I galloped Lordy on such a wet day. I ease the horse off the rail, and he slows, his breath coming in sharp snorts.

Still galloping, the bay filly goes an extra few strides before moving off the rail and gradually slowing down. We catch up and then keep pace as the horses wind down like giant mechanical toys. I concentrate on each stride, trying to feel where the problem is. Lordy is cantering now, and I let the reins out a little. As long as he's quiet and relaxed, I don't mind letting him have a bit of a stretch. We reach the turn again, and Lordy switches leads. Then he switches back again. Does it mean anything? I ask him to change leads again, and he does, but he doesn't stay on the new lead. He switches back and tosses his head, one ear flicking back toward me.

He drops into a trot, and I partially straighten my legs and stand up in the stirrups. Water drips off the back of my helmet. When I change position, a trickle runs down the back of my neck. We have just started walking and turned to the gate when Scampy starts yelling at me from under his ballcap.

"What the hell are you doing up there? This ain't no fancy dressage show."

"What?"

"Don't *what* me. You know exactly what I mean. Freakin' lead changes all the way down the stretch. I don't pay you to make the damned horses dance!"

"I was just trying to—"

"Did I ask you to work on freakin' lead changes? Did I?"

I open my mouth and take in a breath.

"Save it! Get Lordy back to Em and then you can help her clean stalls."

"What about Chiquita?"

"Never mind Chiquita. Jimmy can handle her. Stalls. Do I make myself clear?"

Perfectly clear. No more rides for me today. No more money either. Cleaning stalls is usually up to Em and Tony. That's part of what grooms get paid for. Exercise riders get paid to ride. No more rides today, no more money. It's one thing when I volunteer to give Em a hand. It's quite another when Scampy orders me to do something that's not my job.

I'm not stupid enough to say anything aloud, but in my mind, I have plenty to say to Scampy. None of it is polite.

"What's up?" Em asks as I jump off Lordy. Part of me wants to tell her exactly what I think of her bad-tempered uncle. No matter what I say, it would make me seem pretty bad-tempered myself. "Nothing."

"Em! Get the tack off that horse. Don't just stand there." Scampy must have sprinted to get back to the barn so fast. "Stretch here is going to help you with stalls today. So take your time cooling out Lordy."

Em looks from Scampy to me and back to Scampy. *Stretch?* she mouths. It's a new nickname, and I have the sickening feeling it's going to stick. Then she moves into cooling-out mode. Smoothly, efficiently, she pulls off the saddle and pad. Off comes the bridle, on goes the halter. On goes a mesh sweat sheet. It's done in seconds.

"Come on, big boy. Let's go for a walk," she says. Em turns to go back out the way we just came in. Lordy turns neatly in a circle around her. He's sweating and still breathing hard after his workout. As they walk away, I watch, trying to detect any sign of lameness.

"Keep him under the covered walkway," Scampy calls after Em. She lifts an arm to indicate she heard. Then she and the horse disappear around the corner. All the shedrows are joined up with covered walkways— it's possible to do a circuit of the whole barn area without ever going outside. On a day like this, that's a good thing.

"What are you gawking at, Stretch? Wheelbarrow's where it always is."

"I'm going."

Scampy doesn't comment on my tone of voice. The tack-room door bangs shut behind him. Despite the fact my stomach is twisting with hunger, there's no way I'm going in there after him to get my sandwich out of the fridge.

I grab a manure rake, a broom and the wheelbarrow and set to work. My Mp3 player is in the tack room. I can't even crank up the volume to drown out the rain hammering on the roof, the blood roaring in my ears.

I strip two stalls and steel myself for a sprint through the rain with the barrow piled high with shavings and horse manure. Just then Tony saunters down the aisle.

"Don't trip, Stretch," he yells after me as I slosh out through the puddles. It's a good thing he's behind me and doesn't see me pull a nasty face. It takes about ninety seconds to get from the back end of our row of stalls to the manure pile and back. By the time I jog back inside, I am drenched.

"Having a good day, Stretch?" Tony asks.

I don't trust myself to speak.

We both turn when we hear Lordy clip-clopping down the aisle. Em puts him back in his stall and says to me, "We're worming today, Stretch."

Could this day get any better?

The next thing I know, I'm staring at the closed tack-room door. Again.

Tony slaps me on the back. "Guess she's not sharing her lunch with you today."

"Whatever."

Tony starts to laugh, but is overtaken by a wicked cough.

"Why don't you go suck on another cancer stick?" I ask.

Tony's left hand shoots out and cuffs me on the side of the head.

"Get lost!" I say, grabbing my ear.

"Suck it up, Stretch. Nobody wants to hear your whining." With that, he deliberately reaches into the back pocket of his jeans and pulls out a pack of cigarettes.

"I'm stepping outside for some fresh air. You don't have a problem with that, do you?" Tony's other hand curls into a fist. I don't say anything. Jerk.

Bang. Bang-bang.

The tack-room door slams open and Scampy charges through. "Stop with the bloody kicking!" he yells at Devil May Care. The horse still kicks for no good reason. Scampy will put up with pretty well anything the horse does. Devil May Care is blazing fast.

Devil pops his head over the rubber stall guard.

"I'll deal with you later." I'm not sure if Scampy's talking to me or to the horse. He storms off down the aisle, turning his jacket collar up and tugging his ballcap down low over his ears. Em appears in the tack-room doorway.

"You coming in? Or did you eat already?"

I turn to give Tony my best *screw you* look, but he has disappeared.

"Where's Scampy going?" I ask Em.

"Feed store. Well? You coming? All the heat's escaping."

"I'm coming. I'm starving."

Inside the tack room, I peel off my work gloves and hang them up over the space heater. I take a deep breath and push aside all thoughts of the pounding I'd like to give Tony. Em and I have at least half an hour before Scampy gets back. There's no way I'm going to let Tony get in the way of me enjoying a few minutes of hanging out.

"This is June! How can it be so freezing?" I rub my hands together and unzip my jacket.

"Grape?"

Em holds a plastic bag of purple grapes out to me. A peace offering. They probably have seeds. I take one anyway.

"Thanks." I should leave it at that, I know, but I can't stop myself from asking. "So, how was Lordy when you cooled him out?"

"Are you still on about him being sore? He's not sore. He's fine."

She pulls the bag of grapes back and cradles it against her stomach. The temperature in the room feels like it just dropped ten degrees.

Em leans her head against the back of the truck bench. "You think I wouldn't notice if something was wrong with him?"

I don't say anything. There's no question she knows her stuff. Knows her horses. She practically lives at the barn.

"I spend more time with that horse than anyone. You ride him for—what?—five minutes a week?"

It's more than that, but I'm not going to argue.

"There's no heat. No swelling. And he was fine when I walked him. I'm going to ice him after this"—she waves the bag of grapes at me—"and then wrap him. If there is something bugging him that he's not telling me about, that will take care of it."

"Em, I know what I felt."

"What did you feel, Mr. Expert?"

What *had* I felt? Anything that couldn't be attributed to the mud and an off day?

Have I just ridden the horse on his bad days?

"You know he had his feet done yesterday?" Em asks.

And, yes, sometimes a horse will be a little sore for a day or two after getting new shoes.

"Forget it," I say. "You're probably right." It takes me all of three minutes to bolt down my sandwich and guzzle a cup of stale coffee. Em offers me another grape, and then she pulls out a carton of worming paste.

"Ready, Stretch? This should be fun."

chapter nine

Worming Scampy's horses is never exactly fun, but it's not the worst job at the barn. As always, Em is efficient. In a pail, fourteen individual doses in separate tubes are uncapped and ready to go. I grab the halter and lead rope from the hook outside the stall door. Then I duck inside and slip the halter on the first horse, Bananorama.

Meanwhile, Em dials back the little wheel that measures the dose on the worming paste dispenser. By the time she's done that, I have Bananorama turned around in the stall so her back end is pointing into a corner and her head is away from the door. That way, she can't go backward and is less likely to plunge forward and try to get out past us.

Em slips under the stall guard, and I hang on to the horse's halter. Em slides the dispenser into the side of Bananorama's mouth, aiming toward the back of the tongue. She presses the plunger and wiggles the tube from side to side to smear the paste around.

Not bad. We're in and out in under two minutes.

Unfortunately, most of the horses try to make the job difficult.

The worst is Chiquita. She throws her head straight up and jerks it from side to side. The worming tube flies through the air and lands in Chiquita's water bucket.

"Get a better hold of her, would you!" Em says. She fishes the tube out of the water and dries it off against her jeans.

"Bucket?" I suggest.

Em scowls at me. She hates it when I try to tell her how to do her job. Whenever we try to worm Chiquita, Em figures she'll outsmart the filly without needing the bucket. And, every time, Chiquita is an idiot. After a short tussle with a stubborn Chiquita, Em sighs and fetches a bucket. She turns it upside down and stands on it. Between me hanging onto the halter and Em balancing on the bucket, Chiquita loses the worming battle every time.

Then Chiquita moves on to the second part of her defense. She refuses to swallow. Instead, she holds the glob of nasty paste on her tongue and purses her lips. Em and I take turns stroking the filly's throat, holding her mouth shut and lifting her head up. The minute the paste is in her mouth, she shoves her head so low her chin scrapes the ground. It takes two of us to heave Chiquita's head up to stop her from spitting out the medication. Eventually, the saliva must build up in her mouth, because finally she gives a huge sigh and swallows. The muscles of her gullet ripple as the blob of worming paste and about a gallon of horse spit slide down her throat.

When it's Lordy's turn, he clamps his teeth shut tight and pokes his nose down toward the shavings.

"Come on, don't be such a wimp," Em says, smoothly sliding the tube into the side of his mouth, forcing it between his rubbery lips. She depresses the plunger and delivers the dose right where it's supposed to go. "You'll run faster next week if you don't have a belly full of passengers."

"Run?"

"Run. Race. He's a racehorse. That's what he does."

"He's racing again next week?"

"Spencer, leave it alone. He's running. He's fit. He's fine. And this time, get your grandmother to bet on him. She's a pensioner. You're supposed to be helping her pick winners."

"She told you what happened?"

Em rubs Lordy's shoulder when the horse swallows and slips him a piece of carrot from her back pocket. He bobs his head up and down like he's agreeing that carrot tastes way better than worming paste.

"You were riding when she dropped off your lunch. Last week, I guess. She wanted to know how Lordy was feeling."

Now my own grandmother doubts my judgment?

"So I told her. The horse is good to go."

Em runs her hand down Lordy's legs, one at a time. She gets a look on her face that's far away and totally in tune with the horse. I love that look. For some reason it makes me want to bend over and kiss the back of her neck.

"No heat. No swelling," she says to me. Then she adds, "I'll be back to slap some mud on those legs, okay, big boy?" She rubs Lordy in a spot right behind his withers. "Look at his lip." She grins as Lordy's upper lip begins to wobble with pleasure.

He looks happy. I wish a rub between my shoulders was enough to change my mood.

"Who's next?" Em asks, ducking under the stall guard and fishing out the next dose of wormer.

"Take it easy, Lordy," I say, giving the horse a rub between his ears as I take off his halter. Devil May Care wallops his stall wall with a mighty kick next door. This should be fun.

Against all odds, Devil May Care is easy to worm. He barely moves when Em slides in the tube and squirts the paste into his mouth. His eyes get a little bigger and he lifts his upper lip, flashing his teeth and gums after he swallows, but he doesn't actually do anything bad.

"Who would have thunk it?" Em says, giving Devil an extra long scratch on the neck. "What a good boy. You could teach some of these other horses some manners."

Em keeps on scratching, and Devil keeps his upper lip pulled way, way back, so he looks like he's grinning. Sometimes I think that's what horses do best—fool us and then chuckle behind our backs.

chapter ten

"Was that your last one?" Grandma asks. I drop my backpack on the floor and flop onto the couch.

"That's it for this year." Exams. I have two more years of high school left. I have no idea how I'm going to survive.

"We should go out for dinner, maybe invite your mom."

"Hmm."

"That doesn't sound very enthusiastic."

Grandma gives me a long, hard look. "Is your report card going to be that bad?"

"Hmm."

"Grunting is for cavemen. You may as well tell me. I'm going to find out soon enough."

"I dunno."

"Why is it that when you talk about school you mumble?"

I shrug.

"*B*s?" Grandma is nothing if not persistent.

"Maybe one, in art. Oh, two. I did okay in gym." I notice she doesn't even start with the *A*s.

"*C*s?"

"Maybe in math. Depends on the exam."

"That's it? Only one possible *C* in your real subjects?"

"Art is real."

To her credit, she doesn't push it. There isn't much point, really. "I don't think I have any *F*s," I add quickly.

"Well, that's something, I suppose." She rubs her thumb back and forth under her chin. "I think we should go out for dinner anyway. Would you like to invite your mother?"

The couch feels soft and warm, the kind of place I could happily stay for the next twenty years. At least until people forget about asking what kind of grade I got in grade-ten English.

Grandma reaches over and pats my arm. "It's all right, love. We can go by ourselves a little later. I'm sure your mother will want to see you after the report card arrives in the mail."

I'm sure she will. My head falls back, and I close my eyes. When Mom finds out how badly the last semester went, who knows how she'll react. A major melt-down, I'm guessing. Maybe we shouldn't meet anywhere in public until she's finished screaming at me. Grandma must be thinking along the same lines because she says, "We'll have her over here for coffee. But right now, go toss your bag in your room and think about where you want to go and eat. The new issue of

Blood Horse arrived today. We can look at it over dinner."

Why, I wonder, can't they have interesting stuff like *Blood Horse* magazine to read at school?

The best thing about summer is that I can basically live down at the track. I get there just before dawn and stay as late as I can.

There's always something to do. Between riding regularly for Scampy, helping Em and picking up extra rides for other trainers, I don't have much spare time.

Sometimes, when it's quiet, I slip into a horse's stall and just stand there. There's nothing as soothing as the rhythmic *crunch, crunch, crunch* of a horse chewing its hay. Which is how I find myself in the back corner of Bing Bang Bong's stall, taking a mental-health break in the middle of the afternoon on the first day of summer vacation.

Bing is a hay dipper. He tugs a mouthful out of the hay net and then dunks it in his water bucket. He swishes it around and then lifts his head to keep chewing. Bing repeats this for every single bite of hay. This might make his dry hay easier to eat, but his water bucket is always disgusting.

A noise in the aisle catches my attention. Lordy's stall is directly across from Bing Bang Bong's. Tony stops in front of Lordy and looks up and down the aisle. He hasn't noticed me in the corner of Bing's stall.

Tony takes Lordy's halter from the hook and disappears into Lordy's stall. "Easy, big fella—stand still. There...good...good. Okay—all done."

I hear him give the horse a pat, and then Tony emerges from the stall. He has a bright orange syringe cap clamped between his teeth. After he latches the stall door, he sticks the cap on the syringe and shoves it into the back pocket of his jeans. Then he strolls away, whistling softly.

It's only when I let out my breath that I realize I had stopped breathing.

What is Tony giving Lordy? Lots of supplements and medications are perfectly legal. Many drugs have to be stopped a certain number of days before a race. It's Wednesday. Lordy races on Saturday.

I wait until I can't hear Tony's whistling before I peer out of the stall. I'm alone. I check the white board in the tack room. Nothing is written in the meds column. Tony has worked for Scampy longer than I have. Surely Scampy must know what's going on? How am I going to find out without getting fired again?

chapter eleven

Later that afternoon I help Em drag everything out of the tack room and into an
empty stall.

"Were you here last year when we did
this?" Em asks, pushing a wisp of fine hair
off her forehead. It's all I can do not to
reach over and brush it away for her. "What?
Have I got dirt on my face?"

"No, I just—"

Of all people to save me from death
by blushing, Grandma comes around the

corner and stops in the middle of the aisle.

"What are you two up to?"

"Painting the tack room," Em says matter-of-factly. "It's a summer tradition."

"Oh, right. Wasn't that one of the first jobs you had to help with when you started here last year, Spencer?"

How could I forget? I was terrified of Em and her famously grumpy Uncle Scampy. I'm not scared of Em any more, but Scampy? That's different.

"Where's your uncle?"

"Around. He doesn't like to get too close to this kind of stuff," Em says airily. She waves one slender arm in the direction of the stacked buckets, piled-up milk crates and the upended truck bench. "Too much like work. Check the café. He's probably got his nose stuck in the Conditions Book."

It's a funny thing, but every time anyone refers to the book that lists all the upcoming races, I get a strange squeeze of jealousy in the pit of my stomach. Is it weird, or what, that more than anything in the world I'd love to own and race my own horses? Like Scampy, Dad made most of his money training other people's horses. He also liked to have one or two of his own in the barn. If I had a horse of my own and a couple of good clients, then I could be the one sitting in the Backside Café with a mug of coffee and a pen and my training notebook. I'd figure out who was going to run and when, and which horse had the best chance in which race. Just like my Dad used to do.

"You want to take a break?" Em asks, looking from me to Grandma.

"No, I'm fine."

I don't know why Grandma wants to talk to Scampy, and I tell myself I don't care. I can guess, though. She's probably going to ask him about Lordy and his chances on the weekend.

Lordy's going to be in a race for horses three years and older that haven't won a race this year. His strong finish a month ago means he's eligible but will leave the gate with shorter odds than last time. The race handicappers will have noticed how he's been doing. Depending on what other horses are in the race, he might even be a favorite at post time. Lordy definitely won't be a long shot.

The purse is decent: $25,000. The race is part of a series sponsored by a local bank. The prize money is split between the top six horses, and the winner's share would go a long way to covering Scampy's operating costs.

"I brought you two some dessert to share later—chocolate cake." Grandma stands in the open tack-room door and gawks. "Where's the fridge?"

Em laughs. "Down around the corner out of the way. Just outside the feed room. Follow the extension cord!"

Grandma disappears, and Em plops down on a hay bale and wipes the back of her forearm across her brow. "How did it get so hot? It was, like, yesterday when we were freezing our butts off. We have to get the fans going."

I want to sit down on the bale beside her, but suddenly the bale looks too small for two. Not that long ago I would have plunked down beside Em. We might have had a contest to see who could push the other off the end of the bale. Last summer, when it got hot in the afternoons, we went out behind the shedrow and hosed each other off in the horse wash rack. I'm tempted to suggest we do that again, but Em will guess that even while part of me might be cooling off, her wet T-shirt was going to heat things up in other areas. She'd kill me. The silence hangs in the air between us.

"Break's over." Em springs to her feet. She strides back into the nearly empty tack room and gets back to work.

We work steadily for hours. We sweep the floor and scrub the worst of the filth off the walls. Then we slap a coat of fresh paint over the walls and wooden shelves.

The breaks we take are filled with the endless chores around the barn. We top up water buckets, measure out the grain and supplements for the afternoon feed, stuff hay into hay nets and sweep the barn aisles. We are busy, but not busy enough to stop the questions in my head. What did Tony give Lordy? Why would Scampy risk his reputation doping an average horse? It's not like Lordy is ever going to be a stakes contender. Can I trust Em? Should I tell her what I've seen? She worships the ground Scampy walks on. I can't tell her.

"What? Sorry—"

"I asked if you were hungry."

I wonder what else Em might have said while I was on another planet.

"Do you want to grab something to eat before we put everything back in?"

My gut responds with a loud rumble.

"Okay, then, let's go." She laughs. "Try not to spook the horses with that disgusting noise!"

We turn together and, with a final look back at the horses peeking over their stall guards, we head for the café.

On Saturday morning, Em and I watch Lordy's race from our usual place. It's not far from the tunnel where the horses cross under the track to the paddock, which is the area where they are saddled and the jockeys mount up before the race.

"They're off!"

We can't see the starting gate over on the far side of the track, but we can hear the announcer calling the race and we can watch the start on the big screens above the odds board.

Em starts yelling encouragement when Lordy takes an early lead. "Go, Lordy! That's my boy! Keep it up! Watch on the outside! Gooooo!"

Em bounces up and down as the horses take the far turn and bear down on the homestretch in front of the grandstand. From the start, Lordy has been pushed by a chestnut gelding who has stayed tucked in at his outside flank. From a distance, it looks like the other horse has his nose stuck to Lordy's saddle cloth. I know they aren't quite that close, but the chestnut isn't giving an inch. A gray is making up ground fast and charges up around the outside of both Lordy and the gelding. The gray colt's jockey glances over his shoulder and goes to the whip. The chestnut surges past Lordy and suddenly the race is now between the gray and the chestnut. Lordy falls back, and I can see the rest of the field closing the gap behind the leaders.

Beside me, Em is nearly having a heart attack. She's leaping up and down, bellowing, "Run! Lordy! Hang on, baby!"

And, somehow, he does, making it over the finish line in third place, just ahead of the number four horse, a dark bay wearing the pink and gray racing colors of Jess McKay.

"That's okay," Em says. "We'll make a little money on that one. Let's go!"

We start the long jog to the backside, wave at Jo-Anne at security and are ready to cool out Lordy after he gets back from the drug-testing shed. The winners are always tested, but a second horse is also randomly chosen. Today, Lordy's number came up—again. That's twice in a row. I wonder if someone in power is suspicious.

Grandma arrives back at the barn about five minutes before Lordy. She's grinning, so I know she had money riding on the race.

"Well done!" she says, beaming at us. As if we had anything to do with it. Grandma opens her purse, peels off a few bills and hands them to Em.

"I love that horse," Em declares.

"You had a bet on Lordy?"

"Of course I did," Em said. "Didn't you, Stretch?"

It's a dig, and I know it. I refuse to rise to the bait.

"He was fading fast at the end," I point out.

"He hung in there exactly long enough."

True. But why? Just what had Tony given him?

Em tucks her winnings into the back pocket of her jeans and smiles at Grandma. "That was excellent chocolate cake the other day, Mrs. Sheldrake."

Grandma smiles back. "Glad you enjoyed it. I'm stopping at the farmer's market on the way home; it's cherry season," Grandma says.

Immediately, my mouth waters. Fresh local cherries. With our long wet spring, they were late this year, but oh wow! How sweet they are!

"I was thinking cherry pies...cherry tarts..."

"Sign me up!" Em says.

"As long as Spencer here doesn't get at the cherries before I have a chance to bake."

"Em!" We all turn when Scampy barks out her name. He's leading Lordy, who is jigging and prancing beside him. There's no doubt about it, the horse looks pretty good.

Em doesn't need to be told what to do, and neither do I. I take the reins from Scampy, who turns to my grandmother and says, "Joyce, good to see you. Lordy ran a good race. I'm pleased. Come inside. How about a lemonade?"

They disappear into the tack room and leave us to the long process of cooling out the sweaty horse.

Lordy is drenched, and his sides still puff in and out. Once the saddle, saddle cloth and bridle are off and the halter and sweat sheet are on, we start walking loops around the barns. Each time we pass through Scampy's barn, Lordy visits the water bucket.

"Easy, big guy," Em says when we arrive at the water bucket for the first time. Lordy doesn't listen. He plunges his mouth into the water and takes a huge swig. Two swallows, and then Em makes him move on. We walk another loop and then let him have two more sips. Left to his own devices, Lordy would empty the bucket in one go. And, chances are, it would make him very sick.

With each loop, Em checks Lordy's breathing, how he's moving and whether he's cooling out okay. She slips her hand under the sweat sheet and reaches forward to feel his chest.

Lordy is still wet with sweat and warm when Em says, "Bath time for Lordy."

She coos as she leads him into the wash rack out back.

Lordy knows the routine. It's so great working with an old trooper like him. He happily lets us clip the snaps to either side of his halter and stands quietly in the wash rack. Even so, I keep the lead shank on and stay near his head while Em hoses him down. She starts with his legs and works her way to the rest of his body. A bucket of warm water and horse shampoo are next, and she lathers him up. After a rinse and a squeegee, Em throws a light cotton sheet over him.

Then we walk again. Around and around the barns we go, letting the sun do the work of drying off the horse. As we walk, Lordy's legs loosen and stretch, and by the time he is ready to return to his stall, he is good and hungry and ready for a rest.

chapter twelve

That night my usual nightmare takes a
new direction. In the dream, my dad
is loading a horse into the starting gate.
Everything seems to be going smoothly.
I realize the horse is Lordy. I know something is wrong, but at first I don't know
what. Then I notice that Lordy only has
three legs. Where his right foreleg should
be, a bloody stump sticks sideways out of
his shoulder.

With the stump sticking out, the horse won't be able to squeeze into the narrow stall in the starting gate.

"Stop! Dad! He won't fit!"

The words are loud inside my head, but for some reason my dad can't hear me. He moves behind Lordy, waving a big hook at the end of a stick.

"Dad!"

Dad swings the hook over Lordy's back. He tears a strip of flesh from the horse's back and flicks it back and forth. Blood sprays everywhere. Lordy's ears pin flat against his neck.

"Stop! He won't fit!"

Lordy tries to move forward, but his stump thuds against the back of the starting gate. Dad moves closer, and Lordy lets go with both back legs.

Boom.

The force of those powerful haunches drives both back hooves into Dad's face. His face collapses like it's made of soft clay. His eyeballs explode. His nose and mouth disappear. Flecks of blood and brain spatter everywhere. He falls. All around, horses' hooves stomp and thump. Bits of brain bubble and ooze out of the gaping hole where Dad's face used to be.

"Stop!" I scream, and this time my voice is loud enough for everyone to hear. The horses kneel and melt into the ground. I run to where my dad has fallen and reach out to touch his shoulder.

"Dad?"

Dad's back arches. He bends backward, pushing his head into the soft dirt of the track. His legs kick and push and his arms start doing something like the backstroke. Dad drives himself into the ground. His head, his neck, and then his shoulders disappear. Thrashing and contorting, his legs lift off the ground.

The earth opens her muddy lips and swallows my dad whole.

"Dad!"

"Spencer—shhh."

Grandma's cool hand smoothes my hair back from my forehead. "Shhh. It was just a dream."

I'm drenched in sweat. At Grandma's touch, my head relaxes into the pillow. Will the nightmares ever stop?

A nightmare of another kind tortures me the next day when I hear my mother yelling out in the driveway. Grandma opens the front door and waves her in.

"Where is he? What the hell does he think he's doing?"

Counting the minutes until she leaves again is what I'm doing. Mom stomps up the front steps. She pushes past Grandma and drops her purse on the floor. "Do you think you can get away with this?" she asks, waving an envelope at me. The report card. "I don't know what to do with you! Say something! Don't you care?"

About what she thinks? No.

Mom turns to Grandma, who has closed the door and is now perched on the edge of the couch. "Ma, how can you let him get away with this? You're supposed to be the responsible adult here. And if you can't handle him, then you should have let me know there was a problem so—"

"So, what, Angel? So you could smack him around? Lock him in his room? Don't smoke in here."

Mom jabs her cigarette back into the package and drops the pack on the coffee table. "Damn it, Ma. You're supposed to be looking after him. That includes making sure he goes to school."

"I do go to school!"

"And what do you do there? Sleep?"

"Angel, calm down," Grandma says. "Would you like some coffee?"

Mom's eyes flick to the cigarettes on the table and she nods. "Sure. Yeah. Why not?"

The entire time Grandma is in the kitchen, Mom is in lecture mode.

"Do you want to wind up in some dead-end job making barely enough money to keep a roof over your head? Is that your plan? Do you even have a plan? How do you think you're even going to graduate with grades like these? You are nothing without a high school diploma. Nothing!"

The best strategy is to keep quiet. I stare at the edge of the coffee table until it starts to wobble and dissolve. I blink and the edge comes back into focus. The worst thing is, I know Mom's just getting warmed up. Me winding up in a dead-end job is not her real worry.

Grandma finally comes back and sets two coffee mugs on the table. "Angel. Do you really think yelling is going to help?"

"Whatever you're doing isn't helping! Have you seen these grades?"

She thrusts the paper at Grandma. "It's disgusting! Obviously, he's not even trying."

Grandma shoots me a look over the top of the report card. "He got a *B* in art and another in phys ed."

Mom jumps to her feet, banging her shin on the coffee table. She lets out a string of curse words and then points at Grandma. "*B*s in art and phys ed? What the hell use is that to anybody? Do you think there are any jobs out there for a high-school dropout who likes to doodle?"

I can't help it. One side of my mouth twitches. She sounds ridiculous.

"You're laughing? You think this is funny? This is not funny. You obviously can't see how serious this is. And you"— she turns back to Grandma—"I trusted you to look after him! Taking him to the track is not—"

Here it comes.

"Angel, sit down." Grandma's quiet voice is scarier than all of Mom's screeching. Mom does what she's told and sinks into the couch. How does Grandma do that?

"Spencer lives here because living with you is not an option." She says this so calmly I think for a moment that she's going to get away with it. But then Mom is on her feet again.

"I'm his mother! Living with me should be the only option! You are doing a lousy job of bringing him up! Look at these grades!" She whips the page back and forth like she's trying to kill flies with it.

"Angel. That's enough! You are in my house. This yelling must stop now." Grandma draws the last three words out and, once again, my mother sits. "I agree— the report card leaves a lot to be desired. But Spencer has always had trouble at school; this is not news."

My mom starts to say something, but Grandma holds up her hand like she's directing traffic. Mom's mouth snaps shut again.

"Screaming at Spencer isn't going to do a bit of good. If you take him home to try to yell at him some more there...well, you know what will happen."

We all know what will happen. I'll walk out the door and be back at Grandma's before Mom has taken a deep breath.

"Spencer." Grandma looks directly at me. "What do you think about all this?"

What do I think about all this? I think my mother is a nutcase. I think I hate school. I think I want to be anywhere but in the same room as my lunatic mother. I think

I want to be down at the track. All I can offer, though, is a shrug. At least the urge to laugh has passed.

Grandma sighs. "I'm getting too old for this."

I look up. I hate it when Grandma talks about getting old. I'd be up the creek without a paddle if anything ever happened to her.

"I could maybe find out about that school that Em goes to..." I'm grasping at straws, but I don't want Grandma to feel like she has to take Mom on alone.

Grandma smiles. "Funny you should bring that up. I was talking to Scampy about Em's school just the other day."

So that's what they were talking about.

"Em? Is that the girl from the track?" My mom says the work *track* like it tastes disgusting.

"Em goes to ALC–the Alternative Learning Center," Grandma says.

Mom's nostrils flare and her top lip curls. "Oh, great idea. The school for bad kids."

Grandma purses her lips and takes in a long slow breath through her nose. "Angel, the program offers a very flexible time-table. There's extra help for the kids in the subjects they have trouble with—"

"Ma, over my dead body. Read my lips: N-O. Spencer has enough problems as it is. Schools like that are where drug addicts and teenage moms and losers go."

"Sounds like the perfect school for me, don't you think?" I say to my mother, who glares at me like I'm some kind of insect.

"Spencer, do you enjoy taunting me?"

I don't. But I can't seem to help myself.

A Beatles tune starts playing in Mom's purse. She reaches down between her feet and fishes out her cell phone. She glances at the display and says, "It's Jerry."

The newest boyfriend. A guy with a bad back who lies around a lot because he's on some sort of long-term disability leave from his job in a warehouse.

"Hi, honey. Sure, I'll pick some up on the way home. No, I won't be long. I think we're about done here. Love you. Bye!"

She snaps the phone shut. "Jerry's waiting. Call me with a plan. Because if you don't have a plan, you need to come home where I can keep an eye on you and keep you away from the track. Because I know it's the goddamn track and all the losers who hang out there that have got you into this mess. That place—" She pauses and the lines around her mouth harden. "That place killed your father. Why are you so determined to follow in his footsteps?"

With that, she sweeps her cigarettes off the coffee table and stalks out the front door. None of us says good-bye.

Grandma reaches over and ruffles my hair with her fingertips. "I'm sorry, Spencer." I don't know why she's apologizing. Mom is an adult. She should figure out how to behave better.

I sigh. For a moment I even think that maybe I should find something else to do. The thought is too strange. How could I leave the track? And what if the worst *did* happen? Is it so bad to die doing something you love?

"It's too bad your mother's way of grieving is so hard on the rest of us. Give her time, Spencer."

Time? How much more time? Why can't Grandma see that Mom was crazy before Dad died? The accident might have made things worse, but no amount of time is going to make her better.

"Don't look so glum." Grandma switches gears. "That school Em goes to might not be a bad idea. Why don't you check on the Internet and see if there's a counselor available during the summer? We should at least have all our facts straight before we talk to your mother again."

I nod. Having the facts straight won't make any difference. My mother looks at me and sees my dad, a man who died when a young horse kicked his face into his brain. His accident and my crummy report card are the only facts she cares about.

chapter thirteen

"So, how'd he feel, Stretch?" Em asks as I slide off Lordy and she takes the reins.

"Ha, ha, ha." Lordy felt like a bomb about to go off. Of course. Today was a walk day for him. Em knows very well the horse is just fine sauntering around the Loop, a two-mile trail that wraps around the outside of the racetrack grounds. It's great for the horses to have a change of scenery. They seem to enjoy strolling down by the river and alongside the big field just north of the track. Lordy had yesterday off—a quick turn-out in the sand pen for a roll while Em did his stall, and then back inside. He was raring to go and would have charged around the Loop if I'd let him.

"I need a drink," I say, heading into the tack room. I grab a can of iced tea and sip while Em gets Twitter ready. I double-check the whiteboard to see if Scampy has added anything since I looked earlier this morning. Good thing I do. Beside *Breeze quick ¼*, he's added *Gate*. That's where we'll start, with some practice at the starting gate. Twitter hasn't been with Scampy for long. She was racing in Alberta and only arrived a few weeks ago.

"Hurry up in there," Em calls. "You know how patient she is!"

Out in the aisle, Twitter tosses her head and paws the ground. "Behave!" Em says, giving the reins a sharp tug. "Come on!"

I refasten my helmet strap and pick up my whip. Em and I spin in place as she gives me a leg up and the filly turns in a tight circle around us.

"Jeez, this horse is a pain!" Em says, holding onto the bridle a moment longer as I pick up the reins and nudge my boots into the stirrups.

Twitter dances all the way down the aisle and out the door at the end of the barn. She walks sideways as we reach the end of the building. She flips her head and lets out a couple of huge snorts.

"Easy, easy..." I draw the words out and keep my voice low and calm. She hardly seems to notice. Her coat glistens with a sheen of sweat as we reach the entrance to the track.

I let her trot and then canter a slow couple of laps. Then we make our way to where the starting gate stands ready at the end of the track. Several other horses walk circles in the area behind the gate, waiting their turns to load.

The starting-gate crew works quickly and calmly to load one horse into the gate. The starter makes notes on a clipboard. Horses that don't load safely aren't allowed to race.

When it's our turn, one of the assistants at the gate slides a length of webbing through the bit ring and leads us forward. Two others link arms behind Twitter. She tosses her head, but doesn't make too much of a fuss until the padded doors are pushed closed behind her. We're trapped inside a narrow chute barely wide enough for a horse and rider. We can't go forward until the starter opens the doors at the front. We can't back out after the guys lock us in from behind.

Without warning, a thousand pounds of pent-up racehorse energy explodes. There's nowhere to go but straight up. On both sides of me, the guys scramble to help calm the filly.

Twitter's sides heave, and she thrashes back and forth. Then, it seems like she has settled. I count to three and nod at the starter, who releases the front barrier. In that exact moment Twitter goes nuts again. She launches herself up and forward. Off balance, she plunges out of the gate and loses her footing.

Her shoulder drops. The dirt rises to meet my face. I have a crazy flash of my nightmare, of my head drilling into the track. The next thing I know, I'm flat on my back, staring up into a blazing-hot blue sky.

"Spencer! Jeez, you gave us a scare." Scampy kneels in the dirt beside me. There's a paramedic on my other side.

Spencer. Yes. That would be my name. My head feels like someone split it open with an axe. I reach up and my fingers touch my helmet.

"Lie still, son," the paramedic says.

"I'm fine," I mumble.

Scampy unsnaps my helmet. Someone else takes it off while another person holds my neck still. I realize there are actually two paramedics.

They put a stiff collar around my neck and slide me onto something that's more like a board than a stretcher.

"Hey, I'm fine, really." I wiggle my toes to prove it.

"Better safe than sorry, Spencer," Scampy says. "They'll take you to the emergency clinic and check you over. You'll be back at work in no time."

The paramedics slide me and my board into the back of the ambulance.

"I'll call your grandmother. She'll catch up with you there."

"Is Twitter okay?"

Scampy nods. "That's just what your dad would have said. Raymond always worried about the horse first. She's fine." The ambulance door clicks shut. Scampy's words about my dad are strangely comforting during the short drive to the clinic.

Grandma arrives right after I get back from having my head X-rayed.

"Spencer," she says. "What were you thinking?" She smiles and kisses my cheek. "The idea is to keep the filly on her feet. She'll never win a race coming out of the gate like that!"

"Scampy told you what happened?"

"Do I need to call your mother?" Grandma asks.

"No." I hope Grandma agrees.

"I didn't think so. At least, not just now. I saw the doctor out front. You haven't broken anything."

"Well, hallelujah!" Scampy says, pushing his head through the curtains. "Good help is hard to find!"

Grandma seems to bring out the best in Scampy.

"How's the patient?" Em asks, crowding into the cubicle after Scampy.

"Shouldn't you be feeding some horse?" I ask.

"You want me to leave?"

"Looks like Stretch is feeling better," Scampy jokes. "How long do you have to stay here?"

"They want to watch me for a little longer. But they don't want me here overnight."

"When can you come back to work?" Em asks. Scampy gives her a little shove.

"Get your priorities straight," Scampy says.

Grandma looks from me to Em and back to me. "I think her priorities are straight enough." She looks at her watch and then at Scampy. "I tell you, I'm losing it." She laughs. "In the time it took to walk from the car to here I almost forgot about the parking out there! Do you have change for a twenty?"

Scampy raises an eyebrow and takes a break in his gum chewing.

"I'm in the short-term emergency spot," Grandma explains. "I have to move the car, and the meters only take change."

Scampy's cheeks puff out and he starts chewing again. "It's all wrong, charging for parking at a hospital." He digs in his pockets and gives Grandma a handful of coins.

The curtain swings shut behind Grandma. Em plunks herself down on the bed. Em and Scampy look at me like I'm supposed to say something. So I do.

"Scampy—"

"That's my name. Don't wear it out."

"You know what you said about my dad thinking about the horse first?"

"Yes."

"Well, it's true. I do try to do that."

"I know. I like that about you. The filly is fine. Not a mark on her. Stop worrying about her. Worry about getting better."

"Yeah," Em pipes up. "So you can get back to work."

I swallow hard and push on. "I'm not talking about Twitter..."

"Then what?"

"Oh, Spencer!" Em says.

Surely even Scampy wouldn't fire me in the emergency room.

"I need to know what you and Tony are giving Lordy."

Scampy's jaw drops like I punched him in the mouth.

"Is this about that day you saw me coming out of Lordy's stall?"

I nod. I've caught him by surprise. Maybe he'll confess.

"Spencer, it's lucky you are lying in a hospital bed or I'd smack you upside the head right about now."

Em's back stiffens.

"I would *never*—I repeat—*never* give a horse an illegal drug. Is that clear?"

This doesn't sound like a confession.

"When you get back to the barn, I'll show you exactly what every one of my horses has ever received. I have no secrets. You can check the list. Every last Lasix injection and tube of wormer is written down. And, for your information, that day when you saw me I was taking Lordy's temperature. Is that okay with you?" Scampy has turned a brilliant shade of red. "Jeez, Spencer, what makes you think—"

Then he stops, pulls off his ballcap and runs his fingers through the thinning gray fuzz that passes for hair. He places his hat carefully back where it belongs. "What did you say about Tony giving something to Lordy?"

"The other day he took a syringe into Lordy's stall. I was in the stall with Bing Bang Bong—"

"Stretch likes to listen to the horses *eat*," Em says.

Why, oh, why did I ever mention that?

Scampy doesn't seem to care.

"So Tony didn't see you?"

"No."

"When was this?"

"Wednesday. The Wednesday before Lordy's last race."

Scampy shoves his hands deep into his pockets. He stares at the bed railing. "Hmm."

"What's *hmm* mean?" Em asks.

"Nobody but me or the vet gives the horses medication."

Em's eyes widen. "You won't even let *me* give them anything other than wormer." Em looks at me when she says the last part. I really must have banged my head hard. *Wormer* almost sounds romantic.

"I'll kill him," Scampy says softly.

"No, you won't," Em says.

"Fine. It's just an expression. But I'll fire his ass faster than—"

"Wait," I say. "If you fire him, he'll just do whatever it is he's doing to someone else's horse."

"I'm not going to just stand around and let him dope up my horses!"

I shake my head and immediately wish I hadn't. A wave of nausea washes over me.

"Are you okay?" Em asks, touching my ankle through the sheet. It feels like a jolt of electricity shoots from her hand, through my leg and into my heart. Via my groin.

I shake my head again, hard, to distract myself. The stabbing pain works wonders.

"Please don't do anything until I get back," I say weakly. "Give me a chance to get back to the barn. We can figure out how to get to the bottom of this."

"Get to the bottom of what?" Grandma asks, pushing through the curtain.

"That filly's problem in the gate," Scampy says without skipping a beat. He winks at me. "Stretch here has some interesting training ideas. I'm looking forward to seeing him back at work."

Em checks her watch, and Scampy holds the curtain open. "We've got to run," he says. "Call me when you're ready to come back."

chapter fourteen

Even though I only have a mild concussion, Grandma won't let me go anywhere near the track for five days! The first day, all I want to do is sleep. The next day, I only notice a bit of headache when I really think about it. The next three days are the pure agony that comes with total boredom.

Grandma makes me go back-to-school shopping. We meet the counselor at Em's school, who says I seem like an excellent candidate for their program. Grandma makes me get a haircut.

With all the time off, I have lots of opportunity to think of ways to catch Tony. But when my first day back at work arrives, I'm not exactly sure how to proceed.

When I finally get back to the barn, there's no chance to talk to Em and Scampy. It's crazy busy, and Tony seems to be everywhere all the time.

It's obvious Scampy isn't going to baby me. Don't Mess With Mo is the first horse on my list. He's coming back from an injury. We have to be careful not to put too much pressure on the leg by going too fast too soon. He's doing great, but is taking a little longer than Scampy had hoped to make a full recovery. At this rate, he'll be lucky to race at all this month.

The July sun blazes, and sweat pours down my sides as I fight to hold the tall colt in check. He seems to have other ideas about slow gallops. Even though I hold him well to the outside, he pulls when the other horses roar past along the rail. Around and around we go until we are both drenched and good and ready to call it quits. He's happy and tired and—as far as I can tell, anyway—not in any pain when we make our way to the gate.

I ride four more horses before I'm done and pull off my riding helmet.

"Nice!" Em says with a smirk.

Dragging my butt off the truck seat, I check out my reflection in the cracked mirror on the back of the tack-room door.

"Yikes!"

My hair looks like it's been painted onto my skull. I brush my fingers through my hair, unsticking it from my head. All attempts at fluffing it up fail miserably. A shower here would be so handy.

I settle for the wash rack outside, where I turn on the hose. When the blast of ice-cold water hits my head, I bite back a shout. Frosty, yes, but man, it feels good to drench myself with the cold water. I scrub my fingers through my hair and let the water run over my back, soaking my T-shirt.

When I straighten up, I shake the excess water from my hair and squeegee my face with my hands.

"Whoa! Brain freeze!"

Em, whose face is flushed, looks jealous. I wave the hose in her general direction, and she jumps back. "Don't you dare!" Instead of staying back, though, she marches over, takes the hose, and bends over the stream of water, taking a huge drink. Water dribbles everywhere, and she doesn't make much of an effort to stay dry.

"You coming to the retirement party tonight?" she asks between swigs.

"Bing's retirement party? Is that tonight?"

"Yup. Bing Bang Bong. Going, going, gone!"

"No surprise, I guess."

"Dr. Conrad is coming down to pick him up. She's bringing in a new filly."

"What time is the party?"

"Seven thirty over in the pit. It's a potluck. I'm surprised your grandma didn't remind you. She's bringing pie."

If the party is in the pit, the big barbecue area over near the river, then it won't just be Scampy's barn attending. Chances are, this could develop into quite a big bash. It's strange to be chatting about parties with Em when what we both want to talk about is Tony. I can tell by the way her eyes follow him and then meet mine.

Tony has been lurking around all day. I don't want to tip him off. I try to treat him exactly as I always do. I'm polite, but not exactly friendly.

"I know it's last minute," Em says suddenly. "But if there's anyone you want to invite, that would be okay, I guess."

It suddenly dawns on me that she is thinking I might like to bring a girl. I almost say something, but stop myself. Maybe she's telling me to bring a date because that's what she is planning to do. Maybe she doesn't want me to feel awkward.

"Could you help us get the barbecues fired up and carry stuff over there?"

Now it's my turn to give Em a hard look. If Em is asking me to help get things ready, that doesn't sound like she's got anyone else, like a date, lined up for the job. On the other hand, maybe that's not the sort of thing you get a date to do. Maybe that's the sort of thing you'd get someone who works for your uncle to do. Maybe Scampy asked her to ask me to come early. Em's suggestion that I bring a date might be her way of making sure I know that she isn't asking me to come to the barbecue in anything like a date capacity.

I shake my head, trying to clear the confusion.

"Unless you're not feeling up to it...," she says, misunderstanding.

"No, that's fine. I'm fine. I'll come early." I shake my head again and say, "Water in my ear!"

"I hate it when that happens!" Em says as she finishes coiling the hose. "There's more iced tea in the fridge. I need a drink before we do hay and water."

chapter fifteen

Several hours into the party at the pit, Wee Jimmy is singing a rude song at the top of his lungs.

"Get down off that table," Scampy says, gesturing with a beer bottle in his hand. "I don't need any broken bones. I need you to work tomorrow!"

Wee Jimmy pays no attention. "Have a piece of pie, Jacob," Grandma says, holding out a wedge of cherry pie to Scampy.

Scampy seems to consider whether he should keep on at Jimmy or take the pie. The pie wins. I know how he feels. My mouth waters. I've already had two hot dogs and a piece of pie, but there's always room for more pie. I reach across the picnic table and cut myself another piece.

Grandma swats at my hand, and the precious cargo nearly slides off the spatula before I can get it safely to my plate. "You've already had a piece!" she says.

"Stretch is a growing boy," Scampy says. "Let him eat."

There are two groups of people at the barbecue. Those of us who have no hope of being small enough to be jockeys, and the fine-boned men who look longingly at all the food spread out on the tables. The smells drifting up from the barbecues—roast pork and sizzling steaks and barbecued salmon drizzled in butter and herbs—must drive them nuts. Some of the jocks eat more than others, but it's no secret that those with the biggest appetites pay the price later. They either starve themselves after a big party or find ways to get rid of the food they've eaten.

"I only brought two pies. Spencer can eat pie at home any time he wants."

"I'll share with someone," I offer, though I don't really want to give up a single bite.

Em slides onto the bench beside me. "Like me?" she says, grinning.

Sharing suddenly seems like a great idea. "Here," I say, pushing the plate into the space between us.

We attack the piece of pie from both sides, and moments later only a few crumbs are left. Em takes care of these by licking her finger and sliding it over the plate. She holds out her moist finger, covered with crumbs. "Want the rest?"

"Thanks, I'll pass."

Up on the table, Wee Jimmy is swaying slightly. "Jimmy! Get off that table right now!" Scampy bellows.

"Yes, sir!" Jimmy salutes and sits down in the middle of the table. Two half-empty glasses tip over, and sticky liquids slosh across the table. Two other exercise riders appear on either side of Jimmy and link their arms through his.

"Come on, Jimmy boy, time to go home," one of them says. "I'll call us a cab."

"A fine idea," Scampy agrees. "See you in the morning!"

As the three riders make their way unsteadily toward the parking lot, Scampy says, "He'll be hurting tomorrow."

I'm chuckling when I feel a sharp jab in my ribs. Em's bony elbow pokes me again. She tips her head sideways. "Coming?"

I have no idea where she wants to go. Not that I'm going to argue. "We have some stuff to finish off," she says to nobody in particular. Nobody seems to care.

We head back toward the barns. As soon as we're out of sight, Em grabs my arm. She changes direction and breaks into a jog.

"What are you—"

"Shh. Come on."

Em leads me to a bench overlooking the river. Cool. It's late and I'm alone in the dark with Em. I wonder if she expects me to put my arm around her or something. My mouth goes dry.

"I've been waiting all day to get you alone."

This sounds like a classic "Let's make out" line.

Em, though, seems to have other ideas.

"While you were recovering, I've been watching Tony."

My stomach twists. So *that's* why she wants me alone.

"You are right about him. He's sneaky."

"What did he do?"

"For one thing, when he leaves work at Scampy's, he doesn't always go home."

"You've been following him?"

"How else was I supposed to find out what he's up to?"

I think of Tony's grip on my shoulder and the time he hit me.

"You shouldn't have done that alone. He could be dangerous."

Em laughs. "Tony? He might be a cheater, but I don't think he's dangerous."

I'm not so sure. "So where does he go?" I imagine Em sneaking down dark alleys and waiting outside sleazy bars.

"Not far. He spends a lot of time in Big Joe's barn."

"You're kidding." Not many people voluntarily spend time with the trainer lots of us refer to as Big Jerk. "Why?"

"I don't know. Tony kind of snuck in there when he thought nobody was watching."

"How long did he stay?"

I feel her shrug in the dark. She's sitting very close to me. My arm acts on its own. It stretches out along the back of the bench. My hand settles gently on her shoulder. My chest squeezes. I think I'm going to have a heart attack.

Em shifts ever so slightly closer. She definitely does not pull away. Wow. I nearly forget what we're talking about. When Em speaks again, her voice is softer. Warmer.

"I had work to do. I couldn't hang around. But one day he went to Joe's at least three different times."

"What did he say when he came back?"

"Either nothing, or he'd lie and say he'd been to the café or something."

"Big Joe. I think we need to go to Big Joe's office."

Beside me, Em shivers. "That's what I was thinking."

"When?"

We can hear laughter and music in the distance. The party is still going on over at the pit.

"What about right now?" Em asks.

"Now? Like this minute?" I'm finding it very cozy here on the bench beside Em.

"When else are we going to be here together in the middle of the night?"

She has a point.

"Okay, then. Let's go."

I don't feel nearly as confident as I sound.

Big Joe's shedrow is just like everyone else's. One row of box stalls faces another. A wide aisle runs down the middle. At one end, Joe has converted a box stall into an office by replacing the stall door with a real one.

Em and I are outside the door when she grabs my arm and points. Light shines through the crack under the door.

We both freeze and stop breathing. Low voices come from behind the door. I want to bolt, but Em has a death grip on my arm. She moves—but not in the direction I want to run. Em ducks under the stall guard and into the stall right next to Big Joe's office.

I have no choice. I follow. Inside the stall, a horse pulls its head away from the hay net long enough to give us each a sniff. More interested in food, he turns his attention back to his hay.

The steady munching resumes and, as always, it calms my nerves. Em leans against the stall wall dividing us from Big Joe's office. The walls go up about ten feet. The bottom five feet are built with thick planks, strong enough to withstand a horse's kick. Above that, plywood takes over.

Big Joe hasn't bothered to build a ceiling over his office. Even though the two men on the other side of the wall are speaking quietly, it isn't hard to make out what they are saying. Big Joe's deep voice and slight accent are unmistakable.

"What do you mean we can't do it next week?"

"The damned kid is back." It's Tony. So it's true. He has been hanging out with Big Joe. "And he's patched things up with Scampy."

"Crap. It was good news when the boy got fired. Better news when he got hurt."

"Pansy ass. He'll screw up again and tick the old man off. It's just a matter of time."

"Tall boy. Big nose." The men laugh at this as if it's really funny. I touch my nose. Em smiles. She reaches over, takes my hand and gives it a squeeze.

"What if the horse runs on the weekend?"

"Without a little help? Dead last, would be my bet," Tony says.

"So that could be good. If we do that mare of Roger's this weekend and leave Lordy alone, we can come back to him next time. Long odds are good."

Tony coughs. He really should quit smoking.

"Thing is," Tony says after he hacks up something disgusting, "Scampy is worried about the horse. I don't know how long he'll keep him around if he runs real bad. He's too damned soft on his horses. And that kid keeps going on about how there's a problem. I've heard him talking to Em."

"Hey—we've made our money back and then some. How about we do Lordy once more. Then we move on. Who cares what Scampy does with him after that? That new filly you found has potential."

Tony makes a noise that sounds half grunt and half snort. This triggers another coughing fit.

"It's late," he says when he recovers. "I've gotta go say my good-byes at the party. I've got work in the morning."

The light in the office goes out, plunging the stall into shadow. The only light on now is a single bulb down at the other end of the barn. We press ourselves against the back wall of the stall and listen. The office door bangs shut and Tony and Big Joe head off down the barn aisle.

chapter sixteen

"Let's go," Em whispers from the shadows beside me.

I duck out under the stall guard. Em is right behind me. I reach for the doorknob. Locked. Em grabs the back of my shirt and pulls me back into the stall.

"What are we going to do?" I whisper.

"Up there," Em answers.

I look up to where she's pointing. She wants us to climb over the wall and drop down into Big Joe's office.

"Give me a boost," she says, turning her back to me and bending a leg.

"Are you serious?"

"Of course I'm serious. Hurry up."

I grab her lower leg and knee and whisper, "One, two, three." I lift and she jumps. She gets a good grip on the top of the wall and pulls herself up and over. I hear her drop down into the office on the other side.

I scramble up by climbing on the hay rack and then reaching over to grab the top of the wall. A moment later, I drop down into the dark office beside Em.

"I could have opened the door for you," she whispers.

I'm glad it's dark so she can't see me blush. "That wouldn't have been nearly as much fun," I whisper back. The truth is, I didn't want her to think I was a wimp. Em had climbed over the wall like it was something she did every day.

"Fun? I'm glad you're having fun," she says. "Now what? Should we put the light on?" she asks.

"Too dangerous. Someone might see."

On the other side of the wall, the horse in the box stall snorts. We both jump.

"Did you bring a flashlight?" I ask.

"There's a good idea. Why didn't you think of that before?"

"Me? I didn't know we were going to—"

"Shh. They might have a little fridge in here."

"Why would we care if they have—"

"Shh." Em touches her finger to my lips. "Listen."

Sure enough, we can hear a low hum.

The room is small, and it doesn't take long to find the squat bar fridge. It's against the wall we just climbed over. We're lucky we didn't land on it when we jumped.

Em opens the fridge door and a wedge of light cuts across the floor. It's not much, but it makes it easier to see the desk, a small bookshelf, a TV and a filing cabinet. There's also the usual jumble of buckets and spare bits of tack, a couple of brushes and stacks of papers everywhere. One wall of the office is plastered with photos of naked women Big Joe has cut out of magazines.

"Quit staring. We have work to do," Em says. She starts looking through the papers on the desk.

I look down, into the fridge. Beer. Half a sub sandwich. Something slimy in a plastic container. "I wonder what this—" I reach in for the sandwich container, ready to make a joke about Big Joe's eating habits when I see something behind it. A container with a strange label. I pull it out and read it again to make sure I haven't made a mistake.

"Venom," I say.

"What? I don't even know what we're looking for," Em says.

"I do." I hold the container out to her.

"Venom?" she says.

I open the lid; inside is an unlabeled vial.

"Venom? Does Big Joe have a horse called Venom?" Em asks.

"Not that I know of," I answer. "But I don't think the label has anything to do with a horse's name. I think that's what's in the vial."

"Like poison? He's poisoning horses? But that wouldn't make a horse run faster."

"Don't you remember that trainer in the southern US somewhere? The guy who injected cobra venom into a horse's knee?"

"Oh my god! Do you think that's what they're up to?"

My head spins. I have no idea what they're up to. I have to check on the Internet to see exactly what that other trainer did. If I remember right, the nerve block allowed injured horses to run because they couldn't feel any pain.

I'm not exactly sure why Tony would want to do that to someone else's horse. Messing with a horse like that would also mess with the odds, though. If an unlikely horse ran better, it could pay off if someone knew to bet on the horse. But if this is the game they are playing, and we have found the evidence we are looking for, what do we do next? If we take the vial away, they'll know someone has discovered their secret.

Em has obviously had a similar thought, because she's pulled a syringe out of a box on the shelf behind Big Joe's desk. She pierces the rubbery top of the vial with the needle and draws up a little of the liquid into the syringe. Then she puts the vial back into the sandwich box and the box back into the fridge.

"Quick. Let's get out of here."

The fridge door shuts, plunging the room back into darkness.

Em opens the office door a crack and peeks out. "Let's go."

We slip out and Em reaches back to make sure the door is locked again. Then we move quickly toward the open double doors at the end of the barn. My heart thuds, but I am pretty sure that we're home free. "Em, that was—"

We pop out of the end of the barn and turn together toward the party at the pit. And slam right into Big Joe.

chapter seventeen

"What the—?"

"Joe!" Em says.

"What are you two doing in my barn?"

"Nothing," I say. "We—"

But I don't have time to come up with a good reason for us to have been in Big Joe's shedrow. It's nowhere near Scampy's. Big Joe reaches out to grab my arm. At the same moment, Em bursts into loud hysterical laughter. She grabs my other arm and sways.

"Joe, please don't tell Scamper Bamper Boo..." Em dissolves into giggles and falls against me. Joe and I both reach out to catch her. "Oh my god...Scamperooni would freaking kill me..." Em leans into me. "Right, Stretchie?" A lightbulb goes on. She's pretending to be drunk.

"It's okay, Baby Cakes. I've got you," I say. To Joe I add, "Sorry, Joe. I didn't know where else to take her. We wanted to stay far away from Scampy's..."

Big Joe slaps me on the back. "Hey, I hear you, Buddy."

Em groans and clutches her stomach. "Ohhh...I'm gonna be sick."

She gives a realistic retch and Joe takes a step back.

"Come on, let's go." I drag Em forward. She leans into me and I make a big deal about holding her up. We take a few steps and she drops to her knees. The noises are disgusting. I know she's faking it, but it still makes me feel sick.

"Have fun, kids!" Joe says and heads into the barn. Em stops retching long enough to listen to Joe's office door open and close.

"Let's go," she says. We sprint off and disappear into the maze of barns. We finally stop running and lean against the side of the shavings shed to catch our breath.

"*Baby Cakes*?" she says, gasping.

"*Stretchie*?" I reply.

We look at each other and burst out laughing. We can't stop. Tears run down my cheeks. I can't breathe. The harder I laugh, the harder Em laughs. We laugh until my stomach aches. Em is beside me, her back against the wall. Her head tips back and her eyes close. I turn to face her and take a deep, shuddery breath.

"Em—"

She doesn't wait for me to ask. Instead she leans into me, for real this time. Her lips brush my cheek. I wrap her into my arms and lean down to kiss her. Properly. On the lips. And for a short time, nothing else in the world matters. Not Big Joe or Tony or how the horses might run.

Wee Jimmy doesn't show up in the morning. Scampy is in a sour mood when he rolls in at 5:30 AM, an hour or so after Em and I arrive to start work. We both feel pretty grim. So does Scampy.

"How the hell does he think I can run a business here?" he asks.

We ignore Scampy's string of swear words and keep working. Everything is different and everything is the same. We work just as hard, but Em keeps catching my eye and pulling funny faces. I try not to laugh. Giggling is not so cool in the cold light of day.

Em has told Scampy what we found in Joe's fridge, and as soon as the testing guys get in, we're taking the sample over. Every time I see Tony, I get a strange guilty feeling in my gut. I wonder what the penalty is for trespassing in someone else's barn when the result is finding an illegal drug. If the syringe really does contain anything stronger than vitamins, that is.

I don't exactly have time to dwell on the problem, because Scampy has me in the saddle before the sun is up.

Chiquita Manana is raring to go. We join the other horses making their way to the track for their morning workouts.

I fall into step with Ellen, one of the riders who left with Jimmy.

"No sign of Jimmy?" Ellen asks.

I shake my head and organize my reins.

"He wouldn't let us take him home. We dropped him off at the Bull and Crown."

"I wonder when we'll see him again," I say. The Bull and Crown is a grungy bar not far from the track. Wee Jimmy Jump-up isn't the only person from the track who has disappeared into the bar for a drink and not been seen again for days.

"Ready?" Ellen asks.

We warm the horses up together, and then Ellen peels off to the outside. They aren't going for a fast workout today. I make a kissing sound to Chiquita Manana and the filly responds beautifully. She hits her stride and gallops strongly, her breath coming in great whooshes. I wiggle my whip out to the side, and she accelerates past a chestnut colt heading across the finish line. She pins her ears and surges forward. I let her run well past the line, enjoying the filly's sheer power and easy balance as she navigates the turn. When I feel her begin to tire, I let her slow and gradually bring her back to a canter and then to a big, springy trot. Scampy looks pleased when we reach the gate.

"Good," is all he says. "Lordy's next. Don't push him."

I know what this means. Scampy doesn't want to hurt the horse, but he doesn't want to tip off Tony either.

After I've exercised Lordy, Scampy waits at the gate, pushes his cap back and looks up at me. "Well?"

"Same, Scampy," I say. I look around to make sure nobody is close enough to hear. I drop my voice. "Uneven when I push him."

Scampy nods and then says loudly, "Good! He's a good racehorse, aren't you, big boy?" He reaches up and pats Lordy on the neck.

Tony is over by the fence watching the workouts.

My teeth clench, and I have to force myself to relax my jaw. I can't let Tony know that we know what he's doing.

There's a lull in the action in the middle of the afternoon. Scampy makes some excuse that his back is bugging him and asks Em and me to come with him to the feed store.

In the truck, Scampy says, "You can't hand in that sample."

"What?" Em and I say together.

"Think about it. If you go in and tell them my horse used this stuff—"

Em and I look at each other. Who would believe that the trainer didn't know what was going on?

"But—"

"And we don't know for sure that they did anything wrong or how that stuff got into their fridge." Scampy starts counting on his fingers. "And, we don't know that it's the same stuff Tony injected in Lordy's leg. We don't even know if that's where he gave the shot!" Scampy squeezes the steering wheel and chomps on his gum.

Scampy's right. We have a pretty flimsy case.

"But it's pretty obvious what they're doing," I say. "I looked up venom on the Internet."

Em jumps in. "Cobra venom works like a nerve block. If you inject it into a joint—"

"Yeah, I know. The horse gets temporary relief. He runs better than expected. Place a big enough bet on a long shot and you make some serious money."

Scampy turns onto the highway and stops chewing his gum long enough to merge in front of a semitrailer truck.

"I know how the scam works," he continues. "But that doesn't help."

A few minutes later we pull into the parking lot of the feed store. Scampy shuts the truck engine off.

"What I don't understand is why Tony would bother with someone else's horse," Em says.

A pained expression crosses Scampy's face. "Tony actually owns half of Lordy."

"He does?" Em looks as shocked as I feel. "Really? Since when?"

Scampy nods. "I was short of cash heading into the spring meet, and Tony offered me a fair price for a half share. More than a fair price." Scampy shakes his head and looks like he'd rather be anywhere else. "I owed him a little money—for wages."

He sighs. "Sometimes I hate this business. Tony let me off the hook for the back pay and threw in a little cash to boot. For a horse that wasn't running great..." Scampy leaves the sentence unfinished. I can see how it could have happened that he would have sold half the horse.

"I should have known better. If a deal seems too good to be true, it probably is."

"So Tony is getting a chunk of the purse money?" Em asks.

Scampy nods. "Big Joe is probably getting a piece of the action too. I wondered how Tony found the cash to buy in."

"What are we going to do?" Em asks after all this sinks in. Nobody answers.

The three of us sit side by side and stare through the windshield.

"Crappy situation," I finally offer. "We do nothing and they keep doping horses that shouldn't be running."

"Turn them in," Scampy adds, "and my name is mud. They could say I knew, and then I'll be fined and suspended."

"Your word against Big Joe and Tony," Em says. "Your word would win, wouldn't it?"

"It should," Scampy says. "But I wouldn't want to bet on it. Maybe I should just retire Lordy now. This was going to be his last season anyway."

Em shakes her head firmly. "That would spook them for sure. Why would you retire a horse that is racing better than he has for months?"

Scampy has a good chew while he stares at the feed store. "I can't let him run again. Not if he's hurt." He shoots me a sideways glance when he says it. That's as close as he's likely to come to an apology. Silently, I accept.

"And you two—" He nods in our direction. "Break-and-enter..."

He doesn't need to finish. Cheating at horse racing isn't legal. But neither is breaking into someone's locked office. If anyone finds out what we did, we could be in even more trouble than Big Joe.

chapter eighteen

In the short time it takes to run a horse race, it is impossible to think of anything except what's happening on the track.

Chiquita Manana's chances in the fourth race on Friday are good. Better than good. Grandma has twenty dollars on Chiquita to win. Scampy has a much bigger bet riding on the filly. Em and I each have five-dollar show bets riding on Chiquita, which means we won't make much even if she wins, but we're pretty certain our money is safe.

And we'll get a little something if she finishes anywhere in the top three.

The field is small—only six three-year-old fillies are running. A seventh entry was scratched after the vet said she was unsound.

"This should be good," Em says as we take our places at the rail.

The race is a mile and a sixteenth long. It's also a $20,000 claiming race, which means that someone could buy Chiquita Manana right out from under Scampy. All the new buyer would have to do is deposit the claiming price with the horseman's bookkeeper ahead of time. The name of the horse the buyer wants to claim would be put in a locked box in the racing secretary's office and, right after the race, Scampy would have to hand Chiquita over. Getting a good horse claimed is a terrible feeling, and I just hope it doesn't happen to Chiquita. Scampy hasn't said it aloud, but I think he sees stakes-race potential in Chiquita. I see stakes potential in the little filly the minute the starting gates fly open and she leaps out onto the track.

Em and I start screaming as Chiquita surges into the lead. Ben Jenson is riding, and he eases her along the rail.

"Keep going!" Em screams beside me. She's bouncing up and down already, and the race has barely started.

Chiquita looks like she's relaxed and happy, zooming along out in front. She has opens up a comfortable three-length lead over the next three horses. They are in a tight clump, and as they come around the turn, I wonder if the horse on the inside gets bumped. It's the number four horse, which drops back for a few strides. The number two horse drops down to the rail, and the number four horse is forced to go wide and try to get past on the outside.

Out in front, Chiquita gallops on, oblivious to the drama playing out just a few feet behind her.

Ben Jenson throws a quick look over his shoulder, but nobody is challenging, so he settles back into his crouch and focuses his attention on the track ahead.

"Chiquita! Chiquita! Chiquita!" I scream as they barrel around the final turn and head for the homestretch. The announcer calls the race at a frantic speed matched by the pace of the horses charging past the grandstand.

"Coming into the stretch it's Chiquita Manana out in front all by herself. Back four lengths Sweetandsour and Openandshutcase are neck and neck. Fat Chance is coming up on the outside..."

I can't hear anything else because I am now yelling even louder than Em. "Go, Chiquita baby! Go!" The fence cuts into my chest as I throw myself forward, both arms pumping wildly as if I am on top of the filly, driving to the finish line. Chiquita plunges forward and crosses the line, easily winning the race by five lengths.

"She was pulling away!" I say to Em, giving her a quick kiss. Em throws herself into my arms. "Great race! Great filly!" Em replies, kissing me back.

We jump up and down like two little kids at Christmas.

We run over to the winner's circle, where Scampy and the owner, Samuel Billington, his wife and three granddaughters all pose for the official winner's photo with Chiquita and Ben Jenson. When Ben jumps off after the photos are taken, Mr. Billington grabs his hand and shakes it up and down.

"Wonderful race, Ben. Wonderful race."

"You have a nice filly here, Mr. Billington."

Scampy joins in the next round of hand-shaking and back-slapping. Mrs. Billington snaps some more photos before Scampy bustles forward and takes Chiquita's reins. "We have an appointment at the shed," he says. And he leads Chiquita off for her drug test.

Em and I make our way back to the barn, babbling all the way. We replay the highlights of the race and marvel at how easy Chiquita made it seem.

"Post to post," I say. "She led all the way."

Scampy is beaming when he finally gets back to the barn. Chiquita looks great. Em and I fly into action to get her cooled out. The Billington family hangs around and gets in the way as we pull off the filly's tack and start the long process of walking.

The granddaughters, who are wearing shorts and sandals, don't seem to realize that getting stepped on by a horse hurts like hell, even when you're wearing boots. Their pretty pink toenails look cute, but they don't belong in the barn. Scampy tells them to stay back three times before he finally says, "Let's get out of the way and let these two get your horse cooled out." He leads them into the tack room, and when the door closes, Em and I heave a huge sigh of relief.

The Billingtons have gone when we eventually put Chiquita back into her stall with a net full of fresh hay.

Just as I'm filling Chiquita's water bucket, Grandma shows up.

"Love that filly," Grandma says, poking her head into Chiquita's stall. "I brought her a carrot. Is that okay?"

"Go ahead," Em says.

After Grandma gives Chiquita her treat, she asks, "Spencer, have you talked to Em about school?"

"School?" Em asks. "What about school?"

I feel the blush creeping up the back of my neck and burning through my cheeks. I've talked to Em a lot the past few days. There are two main subjects. What to do about the venom we have stashed in the bottom of my closet. And how cute Em's freckles are.

"We've been kind of busy," I offer, though it sounds lame even to me.

"Are you busy now?" Grandma asks.

"Not for a bit," Em says. "We'll do another round of hay and water later, and a couple of them are getting supplements late. I'll check bandages once more before I leave, but we should really grab a bite to eat..."

"I'll treat you both to a burger at the Café," Grandma interrupts Em's long to-do list.

"Great, thanks!" Em says.

Nobody asks me, but I guess they figure I'm always ready to eat. Which is true.

At the café, we slide into a booth and Grandma asks, "So, how did you two make out?" Em and I catch each other's eye and grab menus at the same time. How did we make out? I'm pretty sure Grandma isn't asking what it sounds like she's asking. "How do you mean?" Em says.

"Your envelopes."

"Ohhh," we say together.

A huge grin lights up Em's face. "We should have got about fifty-four dollars each," Em says, "but because Wee Jimmy still hasn't shown up, we got to split his share too. Uncle Scampy was feeling generous, so we each got eighty dollars."

I love it when a horse in our barn places in the top three. The two grooms and regular exercise riders get to split a barn bonus. It's not much, but over the whole year, those bonuses can really add up. I wonder how much was in Tony's envelope. It must have been hard for Scampy to hand it over.

"You should be buying me dinner!" Grandma says.

"I could—" I start to say, but she waves me off.

"I did very nicely myself," she says. "I had twenty on the filly to win, as you know. But then I also had her as the winner in two exacta bets, and one of those paid off! For a lark I picked the long shot: Fat Chance to come in second. I couldn't believe she snuck in there right at the wire. It was very close for second and third. That was the more exciting race!"

"Way to go!" Em says. It's not easy to pick the top two horses in the right order. It's hard enough to win a bet trying to figure out if a horse is going to come somewhere in the top three!

The waitress comes by and takes our order. When she leaves again, Em looks at me from across the table. "Are you thinking about going to ALC?"

"I had an appointment with the counselor when I was recovering."

Em grins. "That's great! Why didn't you tell me?"

I shrug. "I wanted to surprise you?"

"Turkey." She kicks me under the table, but she's smiling.

"How could I resist a school where I can work here mornings, go in to school for three hours every afternoon and then get back here by four thirty to work some more?"

"It's a great life, isn't it?"

"I'm curious," Grandma says. "What are the other students like? Are they all"—she pauses before adding—"troubled?"

Em rolls her eyes. "Do you think I'm troubled?"

"Oh, yeah," I joke. "You're big trouble."

Em balls up her napkin and fires it across the table. "Yeah, we're all deeply screwed up. You'll fit right in, Stretch."

Grandma laughs. "Thank you," she says as the waitress delivers our drinks. "Well, that puts my mind at rest!"

The subject seems to close with that comment, and we return to talking shop.

Grandma wants to know what we think of the big American-bred chestnut colt who won the Dubai World Cup earlier this spring. All the talk right now is whether he'll also win the Man-o'-War Stakes at Belmont Park.

"He's never run on the turf," Grandma says, "so nobody really knows for certain how he'll handle that. But he's a damned fine horse, and I'll have money on him."

The conversation continues like this right through our meal. Finally Em says, "You coming back to the barn or heading home?"

"You need to ask?" Grandma says, reaching for the bill. "This boy would unroll his sleeping bag in the tack room if I let him! I'll see you later, Spencer."

For the rest of the evening as we do another round of checking all the horses, I put up with Em's teasing about how slow I am, how nobody would ever make a dime if they bet on me to win a race. That might be true, but finishing up the chores beside Em, I feel like I've already hit the jackpot.

chapter nineteen

At three thirty in the morning, not many people are out and about. It's quiet, that time between the end of a late night and the start of an early morning. I ride my bike along deserted streets, enjoying the soft hiss of the tires along the road. It's still dark, though at this time of the year the birds have already begun their symphony of chirps and whistles. They are so loud when I pedal along the edge of the park and down the bike path near the river that

I have trouble believing so many birds could possibly spend the rest of the day hiding. Another, smaller, path snakes away from the main bike path by the river and leads me along the fence marking the edge of Hilltop Racetrack's property. It's only thirty seconds or so before I slow down and wave at Jo-Anne in the security hut.

"Morning, Spencer!" she calls out, and I wave back.

Once past the gate, I pump hard and then lean into the turn along the back end of our barn. I hop off, push the bike around the corner and see the lights are already on. Em is waiting for me just inside the tack room. We're at the barn an hour earlier than usual. That should be plenty of time to put our plan into effect. Em and I have finally come up with a way to nail Tony.

The next shedrow over from ours belongs to Ian McIsaac. He has several empty stalls. One is right behind Lordy. Em and I don't say much—we don't have time.

"Laptop?"

Em nods and asks, "Extension cord?" We both grin because the extension cord is looped over my shoulder. "Flashlight?"

I nod. "Webcam?"

Em nods back at me.

"Good," she says. Let's go."

We head straight for the stall behind Lordy's. Once inside, we slide the stall door shut and turn on the flashlight. I pull myself up onto the hay rack. From there, I stretch up to feel along the ledge at the top edge of the stall wall.

Em passes up the tiny webcam. While I'm fastening the camera to the ledge, Em fires up the laptop. We run the wire down the corner of the stall and connect the two.

"A little to the left," Em says, her face lit by the glow of the laptop screen. "The other left. Point it down a little. There. No, up. Down."

It takes a few minutes, but we finally get the camera angle right. I scramble back down and give Em a quick kiss on the forehead. We've already told Scampy what we're doing. He's going to pretend Em is sick. I'm going to help with chores as well as cover my regular rides. That means Tony is going to have to step up and cover Em's horses too. Lordy's supposed to race on Saturday, so we're hoping Tony will think he can get away with giving Lordy a shot. And when he does, Em will be recording every move from the other stall.

"Hey, Stretch—let's see what Devil May Care can do. That colt has some serious speed."

I nod and take Devil May Care out to do a fast workout. When I get back, Scampy says, "Cool him out, would you? Tony's disappeared."

"Sure."

I look down the aisle, but Tony is nowhere to be seen.

Scampy helps me take off the saddle and bridle. "I'll give you a hand at the wash rack if Tony isn't back by then," he says. "Let me know when you're done."

He doesn't say anything, but I bet he's thinking the same thing as I am. Has Tony gone to get the snake venom? Will Em catch him on the camera?

For once, I'm anxious for Devil May Care to cool down in a hurry. The heat and the fast workout mean there's no rushing. I walk the horse around and around the barns, letting him stop to sip water as he cools down.

At the wash rack, I raise my eyebrows when Scampy joins me. He gives a little shake of his head, so I know that Tony still hasn't come back. I wonder if Em has seen anything.

When Devil May Care has been washed, I take him on another slow lap. It doesn't take long for him to be dry enough to put back into his stall. It was hot last night. The fans are already going full blast.

Tony is nowhere in sight. I decide to risk a quick visit to see how Em is doing. I jog to the end of our barn, turn right and slip into the next aisle.

The stall door where Em is hiding with the laptop is open a little. All the hairs on my arms stand straight up. Something moves inside the stall. I sprint to the door and see that Tony has his arm wrapped around Em. His big hand is clamped over her mouth. Em struggles to get away, but Tony is three times her size. Tony reaches down for the laptop, which is on the ground, half buried in shavings.

All of this information hits my brain in a hurry. It feels like I'm in a cartoon, and time slows down. I launch myself at Tony's back and leap on top of him. Caught off guard, he swings around, still hanging onto Em. His hand slips, and she lets out a scream before he muffles her again.

I pound my fist into the side of his head, and Tony swears at me. I hit him again and again. Tony keeps cursing and reaches back to grab me.

The distraction is enough to let Em spear Tony in the stomach with one of her sharp elbows. His breath hisses out, and he staggers back, ramming me against the wall. The impact crushes me, knocking the air out of my lungs. I gasp but hang on.

Em twists sideways and I hear her land a kick. I reach over Tony's shoulder and grab his nose. I drive my fingers up his nostrils and yank up. He yells and crashes sideways, sending a water bucket flying. Em pops free of his grip and screams. "Help! Scampy!"

A second later, Scampy pulls me off Tony's back. Tony is doubled over, his hands covering his face. Blood drips down the back of his hairy arm.

"What the hell is going on in here?" Ian McIsaac says, crowding into the stall with the rest of us.

"Call security," Scampy says grimly. "And the cops."

Tony struggles upright and lunges for the door. All of us grab hold and wrestle him to his knees.

Red-faced and panting, Scampy says, "I don't think so, Tony. You aren't going anywhere."

Tony does go somewhere. Downtown to the cop shop in the back of a squad car.

Em spends the rest of the day showing off her bruises to anyone who will stop long enough to look. She laughs at how it was a sneeze that tipped off Tony. He snuck up behind her while she was checking to make sure she'd saved the video. With earphones in so nobody else would hear, Em hadn't heard a thing until it was too late.

The video is the talk of the backside. People pop by all day, and Em plays the clip over and over again. Clear as day, there's Tony injecting venom into Lordy's hock.

chapter twenty

"He won't work on a track for a long time," Em says to Grandma a few days later. Em's at our place enjoying a glass of ice-cold lemonade. "Between the fines, the suspension and the assault charges..." Em sighs happily. She's pretty proud of the way she helped stop the cheating. There was enough cobra venom left in the needle to identify what had been in the shot. Tony wasn't very loyal to Big Joe. He made some kind of deal with the racing commission to tell everything he knew about the scams Big Joe was running.

They weren't just doping Lordy. At least two other horses in different barns got the snake venom treatment. They never gave it to any of Big Joe's horses, so they wouldn't get caught.

The other trainers didn't know what was going on. They didn't worry too much, because their horses were running well. Hope and wishful thinking are common traits for people in the racing business.

"What about Lordy?" Grandma asks. "What does the vet say?"

"Looks like bone spavin," I say. "We won't know how bad it is for another three or four weeks. That's how long the effect of the venom lasts."

"Strong stuff," Grandma says.

"No kidding." Em agrees. "Scampy sent Lordy to Dr. Conrad's farm. She's going to look after him and see what kind of work he'll be able to do."

I pick up the story. "Then Lordy's going to After Track, that place where they adopt out retired racehorses to new families."

"Another glass?" Grandma asks, clinking a spoon against the jug of lemonade.

Just as Em nods, someone bangs open the screen door. We all jump. "Expecting someone?" Grandma asks, getting out of her chair.

"Spencer?" My mom's voice cuts through the pleasant atmosphere.

Oh no. "Mom!"

"Who's this?" Mom asks when she spots Em sitting beside me at the table. "You've got yourself a girlfriend?"

The blush creeps up the back of my neck and burns its way to my scalp. Em stands up and sticks her hand out. Mom ignores it. "My name's Em. I work with Spencer at the track."

Wrong thing to say!

Mom's lips pinch together in a tight line. She automatically reaches into her purse to fish out her pack of cigarettes.

"Angel—" Grandma warns. The pack disappears back into Mom's purse. "So what brings you here?"

"I'm here to visit my son, if you don't mind."

It's Grandma's turn to purse her lips. I can see where Mom gets it from.

"And to find out what he plans to do about school."

"I'm right here," I say. "You don't have to talk about me like—" I glance over at Em. She's still smiling sweetly. There's no way to know what she's thinking.

"I'm going to ALC in September."

"The school for bad kids?" Mom snaps back at me.

"My school," Em says, still smiling. Her cheeks must be getting sore.

Grandma clears her throat. "They offer a good program for kids who don't quite fit into the regular system." She glances from me to Em before adding, "They can give Spencer the extra help he needs."

"I'll try it until Christmas," I say. "If my grades haven't improved, I'll transfer back to Reston High."

Mom looks less than impressed.

"And I'll quit my job."

Mom's eyes narrow. "So if you flunk out after the first semester, you won't try to work at the track?"

"Not during the school year."

Mom considers this. "And if you flunk out, you'll move back home with me."

I hear Grandma take a deep breath like she's going to say something. She doesn't, though. Moving home with Mom? Over my dead body. I nod, though, as if I'm considering the possibility. "Okay. Fine."

Mom doesn't exactly smile. She leans back in the kitchen chair. "Good."

Grandma and I have talked a lot about how Mom might react to me changing schools. What I'm not going to tell Mom is that I'll do whatever it takes to pass. There's no way I'm going to fail anything.

Then, without warning, Mom leans over the table and reaches for me. I flinch, thinking she's going to slap me. "Hold still," she says. She doesn't smack me. Instead she smoothes a bit of hair away from my forehead and says, "You are so much like your father."

Her eyes fill with tears, and she blinks. Then her phone rings, and she is instantly transported back into her other life. She pulls her hand back and snaps open the phone.

"Hi, honey, I'm just leaving now. Everything seems fine here. Yes. Yes, I'll be back soon. Oh my god! I've only been gone for—Fine. Ice cream? What flavor? Another video? But you never finished the last—"

She keeps talking as she pushes the chair back from the table, picks up her purse and heads back to her car.

When she's gone, we all let out a breath.

"So now you've met my mom," I say to Em.

Em nods. "When do you plan to tell her you're saving up to buy a yearling at the sales next year?"

"If I value my life? Never."

"There's a difference, you know, between being mean and being unhappy." Em stares down at the tablecloth when she says this, almost like she doesn't want to interfere.

What she says makes sense. It's easier to think of Mom as mean and crazy, but it's probably true that she isn't very happy.

Em looks up and smiles at me. My face relaxes into a goofy grin. It strikes me that I don't have to share my mom's house, and I sure don't need to share her miserable outlook.

Em reaches over for the stack of paper on the table. "Is that the race program?" she asks.

"Sure is," Grandma says. "So, you two, who do you like in the first?"

"No Worries Mon," I say without hesitating. "Just because I like the name."

Acknowledgments

If the dream of some is to run away and join the circus, mine is to run away and join life on the backside. Over the years, dozens of generous souls have opened their shedrows, endured my endless questions and tolerated my scribbling pen. To all of you who work with horses in the racing industry and who have been so helpful, thank you. Thanks, too, are due to Melissa McKee, DVM, who graciously answered my questions about snake venom. Of course, this story could not have found its way into the world without the hard work of the wonderful team at Orca. My editor, Sarah Harvey, deserves a special mention. Without her encouragement and guidance, this book would never have crossed the finish line.

Nikki Tate is the popular author of many books for children, including *Jo's Triumph* and *Jo's Journey*. Nikki (and her collection of goats, ponies, dogs, cats and assorted feathered friends) makes her home on Vancouver Island. Each year Nikki visits many schools to talk about her books, lead writing workshops and perform as a storyteller. Interested teachers can visit www.nikkitate.com for more information.